BLACKWELLS
and the
BRINY DEEP

Other Weird Stories Gone Wrong:

Jake and the Giant Hand
Myles and the Monster Outside
Carter and the Curious Maze
Alex and The Other

————— WEIRD STORIES GONE WRONG —————

BLACKWELLS

and the

BRINY DEEP

PHILIPPA DOWDING

Illustrations by Shawna Daigle

DUNDURN
TORONTO

Cover image: Shawna Daigle
Printer: Webcom

Library and Archives Canada Cataloguing in Publication

Dowding, Philippa, 1963-, author
    Blackwells and the briny deep/ Philippa Dowding.

(Weird stories gone wrong)
Issued in print and electronic formats.
ISBN 978-1-4597-4106-5 (softcover).--ISBN 978-1-4597-4107-2 (PDF).--
ISBN 978-1-4597-4108-9 (EPUB)

I. Title. II. Series: Dowding, Philippa, 1963- . Weird stories gone wrong.

PS8607.O9874B53 2018   jC813'.6   C2018-900291-3
                                                  C2018-900292-1

1 2 3 4 5   22 21 20 19 18

We acknowledge the support of the **Canada Council for the Arts**, which last year invested $153 million to bring the arts to Canadians throughout the country, and the **Ontario Arts Council** for our publishing program. We also acknowledge the financial support of the **Government of Ontario**, through the **Ontario Book Publishing Tax Credit** and the **Ontario Media Development Corporation**, and the **Government of Canada**.

Nous remercions le **Conseil des arts du Canada** de son soutien. L'an dernier, le Conseil a investi 153 millions de dollars pour mettre de l'art dans la vie des Canadiennes et des Canadiens de tout le pays.

Care has been taken to trace the ownership of copyright material used in this book. The author and the publisher welcome any information enabling them to rectify any references or credits in subsequent editions.

                           — *J. Kirk Howard, President*

VISIT US AT

 dundurn.com | @dundurnpress | dundurnpress | dundurnpress

Dundurn
3 Church Street, Suite 500
Toronto, Ontario, Canada
M5E 1M2

For Shawna, who asked for mermaids
— Philippa

For Mom and Dad: thanks for all the crayons
— Shawna

THIS PART IS (MOSTLY) TRUE …

You should know, before you even start this book, that it's a little scary. And parts of it are even a bit weird and strange. I wish I could make the story less scary and strange, but this is the way I heard it, so I really have no choice.

It starts like this (which, by the way, is pretty much exactly how every sea story worth telling begins):

One summer evening a long time ago, two brothers were fishing by the sea. It was quiet, peaceful twilight. Not a breath of air stirred, there wasn't a cloud in the sky, the water was still and calm. Candles were lit in homes that dotted the bay. The lights in the harbour shone, and the lighthouse would soon be lit, too, as darkness fell.

The fish weren't biting, but that's not really here nor there in this particular story.

But it does explain why the younger brother was daydreaming. He sat on the wooden dock and stared out at the peach and golden waves as the sun sank upon them.

He closed his eyes and dreamed about mermaids and pirates, enchanted islands and sea adventures, and what it might be like to go to sea as a cabin boy (since this was in the days of such things). A seagull's cry made him open his eyes …

… and there, on the horizon!

An *enormous black ship*!

It had NOT been there a moment before.

The sails were tattered and torn. Thin, ragged sailors ran along the deck. The sailboat heaved and bucked through gigantic waves. Crested plumes of spray flew from its bow.

Then, a curl of smoke. The ship was on FIRE!

The boy shielded his eyes and stared. The fiery ship sailed full force into the teeth of a terrible storm …

… except there *was* no storm. The sea was calm, the sky was clear. But there it was. A burning ship, fighting a storm in high seas.

"LOOK! Out to sea!" The boy called to his older brother, who at that very moment had hooked a fish, their first and only hope of dinner.

"Do you see it? A ship on FIRE!"

"Quiet! There'll be no dinner if I don't catch this fish!" the older brother snapped. His mother had told them not to come home empty-handed.

"But look! It's a ship in distress!"

The giant ship leaned to one side. The flames spread quickly, soon the whole ship would be on fire …

It's so close, but I can't hear the sailor's cries, the boy thought. *And I don't smell smoke!*

The burning ship drew close to shore. A horrible wooden figurehead stared from the bow: it was half woman, half sea monster!

The name of the ship was carved beside the figurehead: *The Mermaid Queen*.

"We have to call the men!" The boy grabbed his brother's arm, and the fish jumped free of the hook.

"You made me lose dinner!" The older brother glared.

"But it's right ..."

When the younger brother turned back, the fiery ship was *gone*!

"But ... where did it go? I'm telling you, it was right there! A ship on fire in a storm! Going down with all hands!" The older brother marched toward home. But the younger brother stared, rubbed his eyes, and scanned the horizon.

The Mermaid Queen had vanished.

Like it had never been there at all.

The only movement on the water was a dolphin. It leapt high into the air then dove beneath the waves.

Now a storm roiled on the horizon. In moments, big dark clouds filled the sky and rain lashed the houses, docks, and boats at anchor in the harbour.

The boy sat in the rain all night, looking out to sea. His mother couldn't convince him to come in for soup (since his brother never did catch a fish) or for bed. She finally gave up and put a rain cape over her son's shoulders.

He watched all night, until the storm blew away and mild dawn broke over the water. He watched until seagulls flew past to begin their day at sea. But *The Mermaid Queen* didn't reappear. There was no flotsam — no wood, no sailcloth, nothing from a shipwreck — washed onto shore the next day, either.

Finally the next morning, as the sun rose, an old sailor limped along the dock. He stopped in front of the waterlogged boy and balanced on his wooden leg (for this was in the days of such things, too).

"It was a *phantom* ship, son. A *ghost* ship. Destined to sail the seas, forever on fire and forever sinking, for all time. Those who see one at sea are in grave danger," the sailor said. This particular sailor was full of strange sea stories about dolphins that turned into boys, sea spirits, enchanted islands, shipwreck grave-yards, and so on.

Most people avoided him. Or thought he'd spent too much time alone at sea and gone a little odd.

But after seeing the burning ship, the boy wasn't so sure.

Time passed, and not surprisingly, per-haps, the boy never did go to sea. In fact, he became a respected lawyer. He stayed very comfortably on dry land into old age, which he spent among his many children and grandchildren.

He was definitely NOT given to telling stories (as a lawyer, that wouldn't do) or seeing things that no one else could see. But on certain summer nights, when the sun was sinking just so, his family might find him staring out to sea and murmuring: *The Mermaid Queen, The Mermaid Queen* ...

You don't have to believe this story. But just because things are odd or a little strange or unbelievable doesn't always make them untrue. Truth is an odd thing; one person's truth can be another person's lie. That's the most important thing to remember about this story: sometimes things that seem like lies are actually true. And sometimes you never can tell.

That's the spookiest thing of all.

Ahoy, Mates! You'll find a glossary of sailing terms used in this book starting on page 136!

CHAPTER ONE

THE LOST SHELL

There was no reason at all to assume the day was going to be anything but normal. The sky was blue. The winds were light. The water was calm.

William, Jonah, and Emma had sailed across the bay alone before. A few times. Their father was waiting for them at the other side as usual. The whole trip would take a few hours.

On any *normal* day.

William walked along the dock, carrying their food cooler. Behind him, he heard his younger brother and sister arguing. Or more precisely, he heard Jonah annoying

Emma. Nothing unusual there. The twins fought constantly.

"Just put your *magic* conch shell in your sparkly *mermaid* backpack!" Jonah teased.

"Stop it, Jonah," Emma said quietly. She liked the shell. So what? She liked the spiral of it and the sound it made if you put it up to your ear. And her backpack was NOT sparkly. It was green, and she drew a mermaid on it with black ink. What was sparkly about that?

"Don't you want to wear your *magical* shell in your mermaid backpack?" Jonah taunted again. Emma ignored him.

William reached their sailboat, *Peregrine*, and swung his long leg over the lifeline. He stepped into the cockpit with the food cooler, and a huge spider scuttled into the scuppers. He frowned. Jitters. He was always a little jumpy when he was in charge. Especially at first.

He cleared his throat. "Quiet, Jonah. Already fighting and not even on board yet. It's going to be a long day unless you two get along."

Emma shot Jonah a glare. She was definitely not looking forward to spending a whole afternoon with him. For twins, they barely got along. Jonah jumped past her onto the boat.

Their sailboat, *Peregrine,* wasn't big, but it wasn't small, either. It had a big cockpit with a wheel for steering and two benches. It also had a covered cabin with two beds, which on a boat are called "bunks," and a kitchen, called a "galley." It even had a tiny washroom for emergencies, called a "head." Pretty much everything on board a ship had a different name from what it was called on land.

Emma swung her leg over the lifeline …

… and for the first time in her life, she tripped getting onto the boat! William grabbed her before she fell overboard.

But all three of them watched as Emma's conch shell flew out of her hand. Almost in slow motion, the shell arced over the boat. It flew toward Jonah.

Emma would remember the next second perfectly, for the rest of her life.

Jonah could have easily reached out and caught the shell. He was a star baseball player. It would have been easy for him. If he'd caught it, then maybe the rest of the day *would* have been normal.

But Jonah *didn't* catch the shell. Instead, he let it sail past him. The shell landed with a *plop* in the deep water of the channel.

Emma gasped. "My shell!" She turned on her brother. "Jonah, you could have caught it!"

Jonah stood above her on the deck. He shrugged and crossed his arms. He didn't look sorry. Emma took a step toward him. She was eight minutes older. And at almost twelve, she was taller than her twin. She'd started her growth spurt, and he hadn't. She was winning more and more of their fights lately.

"Jonah, you're going to pay," Emma whispered, taking another step forward.

William stepped between them. He was still their big brother, big enough to make them behave. Barely. And he had to take charge, much as he hated sorting out their fights. He couldn't have the twins rolling around on deck, trying to throttle each other.

"Thanks a lot, Jonah," William said, disgusted. "Once again, you never fail to disappoint."

"What? What did I do? It's just a stupid shell!"

"You know it's not a stupid shell. Not to Emma," William said. "And she's right, you could have caught it. Apologize, so we can get going."

Jonah sneered. "No! I didn't do anything!" William and Emma looked at him.

"Suit yourself," William finally said. He turned to his little sister. "Emma, I'm sorry your pirate twin didn't try to catch your shell. I promise you we'll find you another one, and Dad will hear about it. Jonah, you're just mean sometimes, for no reason." William turned his back, hoping they'd listen to him. He busied himself and took the cover off the main sail.

Very slowly, Emma raised her hand and pointed at her brother. "You, Jonah Blackwell, are a miserable, lowlife *pirate*! YOU'RE A PIRATE!" she yelled.

Jonah made a face at her, but he didn't budge. "I'd be happy to be a pirate. I'd be the PIRATE KING!"

"Stop, Jonah!" William shouted. "Can't you just *try* to get along with Emma? We're stuck together for the next few hours. Get your lifejackets on and get ready to leave the dock." He stepped down the ladder into the cabin and came back up with the big binoculars.

"Here Emma, watch for whales," he said. Emma took the binoculars. William was trying to be nice, because unlike Jonah, he *wasn't* a pirate. She put the leather strap around her neck.

Then in total silence, and with plenty of glaring, Emma and Jonah untied *Peregrine* from the dock. William started the motor, and *Peregrine* backed slowly into the channel then headed out into the bay. When they were in open water, Jonah and Emma pulled up the sails and William turned off the motor.

The good ship *Peregrine* sailed along the calm water under a bright blue sky.

Emma could sail with her twin brother, but she didn't have to *talk* to him.

She loved that shell.

She found it in Florida the winter that she and Jonah were eight. All day long, Jonah had teased her that she'd never find a conch shell. It was weird, but she knew he was wrong. So she stayed on the beach until after dark, digging in the sand, searching. She was about to give up when a dolphin jumped in the ocean nearby. She watched it leap in the moonlight then disappear, then … there it was. The perfect conch lay in the sand.

It was almost like a gift from the ocean. The strangest part? It didn't surprise her. She knew she'd find the shell that day, somehow. She'd never told anyone about *how* she found it, though, because who'd believe her?

Emma tried not to think about the lost shell. Or what she might do to Jonah when they weren't stuck on the boat anymore.

Peregrine leapt forward in the gentle breeze, and the Blackwells sailed along, slowly leaving the shore behind them.

William steered. Emma looked through the binoculars. Jonah stared out to sea. Emma swept the binoculars across waterlogged stumps, past geese and ducks along the shore.

Then *she saw it*!

Suddenly, a long hand poked above the water. Seaweed trailed from slender fingers that held …

… *a conch shell!*

Emma stared through the binoculars. The hand — was it webbed? — held the shell above the water for a few seconds. Then hand and shell disappeared with a gentle *splash* below the waves.

Emma gasped.

She looked at Jonah and William, but they hadn't seen what she had.

She just *saw a seaweed-covered hand* poking above the water.

And it was holding her shell!

CHAPTER TWO

THE PHANTOM SHIP

Emma stared at the water. What did she just see?

She peeked at William, at the wheel. She shot a glance at Jonah, who sat on the deck, staring at the horizon. She couldn't tell them what she just saw. They'd never believe her. And besides, if she did tell them, Jonah would tease her all day.

But what WAS that thing? Did she really just see a hand, dripping with slimy seaweed, hold her conch above the water?

She clutched the binoculars and swept them across the waves. Nothing.

It was a perfect blue-sky day. The wind blew the sailboat along. At the top of the mast, *Peregrine* flew her ensign: a beautiful white and grey peregrine (the bird) on a bright red flag.

William steered, Jonah sulked, and Emma stared through the binoculars.

This went on for a while. One thing about sailing is it takes patience to get anywhere. But there was plenty to look at. Birds. The sky. The clouds. The gentle rippling of the waves and the sun sparkling on the water.

Strange, seaweed-covered hands holding a conch shell.

Then ... the marine radio in the cabin suddenly crackled!

"*Peregrine, Peregrine, Peregrine*, this is DaddyOne. Please report, over." The three Blackwells jumped. They hardly ever used the marine radio, since they had a cellphone, but William always turned on the radio at the beginning of every voyage. It was marine tradition and the law. To hear their father's voice suddenly out of nowhere was a bit weird.

"I forgot to text him!" William moaned. "Jonah, grab the radio. Tell him we're under way." William frowned. *How could I forget? It was because of losing Emma's shell! But what kind of captain forgets to send an important radio message?*

Jonah scampered down the ladder into the cabin and grabbed the radio microphone. "DaddyOne, DaddyOne, DaddyOne, this is *Peregrine*. We're under sail, over," Jonah said. The radio crackled again.

"*Peregrine, Peregrine, Peregrine*, this is DaddyOne. What's your ETA, over?"

Jonah looked at William, who looked at his watch. "Tell him estimated time of arrival is midafternoon." Jonah nodded. "DaddyOne, DaddyOne, DaddyOne, *Peregrine* ETA at the dock is midafternoon, over."

"*Peregrine, Peregrine, Peregrine*, have a good sail. See you soon. DaddyOne out."

The radio went quiet, and the three sailors went back to sailing, sulking, and watching.

They sailed along for another hour.

Soon *Peregrine* was all alone, out of sight of land, in the middle of the bay.

"I'm hungry!" William announced finally. "Emma, come and steer." He climbed down into the cabin and handed out cheese sandwiches and water from the food cooler.

They ate in silence as the boat sailed along.

And again, for a long time, nothing happened. Jonah sat on the cabin, not looking at Emma. William steered. Emma looked out to sea with the binoculars. The boat moved gently through the water …

… then three things happened at once.

Emma saw something through the binoculars. A trail of bubbles headed toward *Peregrine*.

"What's that?" she said, standing up and pointing. Something was swimming toward the boat. *It looks like a dolphin*, she thought.

William suddenly noticed a dark, thin line of clouds on the horizon. "A storm's brewing," he said at the same time.

And then Jonah shouted, "LOOK! A SHIP!"

"What the …" William whispered.

Jonah was right! An enormous ship with ragged black sails appeared out of nowhere. A tattered crew ran back and forth along the deck.

A moment before, the horizon had been empty.

"Where'd *that* come from?" William yelled. Jonah ran to the bow to get a better look at the ship. The sun had disappeared behind a thick, dark cloud. William was right; a storm was brewing. And fast.

"It's a *brigantine*!" Jonah yelled. "They don't make ships like that anymore! It must be two hundred years old!"

"More like three hundred," William said in disbelief.

The huge ship bore down on them, much closer than it had been a second before. The ship rocked and dove into a rolling sea. The ragged crew ran across the deck, trying to get the ship under control. The torn sails flapped in the wind.

Smoke curled from the sails.

The huge ship was on fire!

For a moment the Blackwells were too surprised to do anything but stare.

"Emma, the binoculars, quick!" Emma handed them over. William searched along the ship. Sailors ran frantically across the deck. Loose and torn sails flapped in a high wind.

But all in silence.

William scanned the ship and lingered on a horrifying wooden carving, the ship's figurehead at the bow: it was a shrieking mermaid! He read the ship's name carved across the stern: *The Mermaid Queen*.

The burning ship moved fast, faster than it should. It was moving so fast, it was going to hit them!

William swallowed hard. "Both of you, quick, ready-about!"

Emma threw off the foresail sheet and William turned the wheel so *Peregrine's* bow crossed the wind. The foresail flapped, then Jonah pulled the sail across the boat and tied it down tight. *Peregrine* shot out to sea, away from the burning ship.

The Blackwells got their sailboat out of danger.

"Emma, go below and radio the coast guard! Tell them an old ship, *The Mermaid Queen*, is out here, on fire!" William yelled.

Emma was about to scramble down the ladder into the cabin to use the radio …

… when Jonah shouted, "But William, it's *gone!*"

CHAPTER THREE

STORM-AGEDDON

The Blackwells stared.

Jonah was right. *The Mermaid Queen* WAS gone. The horizon was empty. They were all alone, except for a dolphin that leapt high into the air then vanished below the waves.

William turned in a circle in the cockpit. He swept the binoculars across the sea.

Nothing.

"But where did the ship go? It was right there!" Jonah said. William handed the binoculars back to Emma. He looked really worried.

"Well, it's gone now," he said quietly. Big, black clouds were closer. The ugly storm was heading their way.

"But what *was* that? That ship almost cut us in half!" Jonah demanded.

"I don't know, but it didn't hit us. And it's gone now, so let's try to forget it," William said. He struggled to keep his voice calm. Even in the few moments since the burning ship vanished, the storm was closer, the waves wilder, the wind higher.

"How exactly are we going to *forget it*, William? We just saw a three-hundred-year-old *brigantine ship* disappear before our eyes! And it was ON FIRE! Now there's a storm coming!" Jonah was yelling now.

"Look, I said it's nothing! Leave it, Jonah!" William yelled back.

"I know what it must have been!" Jonah said, excited. "It was a *phantom ship*! Dad told me about them. Sailors tell stories about them. A phantom ship is an ancient, cursed ship doomed to sail the seas forever. There one second and gone the next."

"Stop it, Jonah! No talk of phantoms!" William shouted.

"It's never a good thing when a crew sees

a phantom ship! They always get caught in a storm, or shipwrecked, or both," Jonah yelled back. The boys stood nose-to-nose. Emma got between them.

"Stop it! Who cares about the ship? Whatever it was, it's gone now! There's a storm coming! We have to get ready!" she said. Her brothers stopped yelling and looked at her.

"William, I have to tell you something," Emma said, struggling to keep her voice calm. The wind was picking up, and *Peregrine* rocked and bucked in a stormy sea.

"Unless it's about the storm, can you tell me later?"

Emma wanted to tell her brother about what she saw. The burning ship was weird enough. But there was the shell. The hand. But what would she say? *There was something out there, holding my shell?*

And who'd believe her? She wasn't sure she believed it herself.

William called out orders, too busy to listen anyway. "Jonah, call Dad on our cell! Tell him we're heading back to shore, there's a freak storm. He should drive home and meet us there. Emma, get our rain gear!"

Jonah jumped below into the cabin and found the cellphone. Emma ran to the hanging locker and yanked out three sets of rain gear.

"It's okay," William was saying. "We'll get wet, that's all. We've been through storms before." What he didn't say? *We've been through storms with DAD before. Never with just ME in charge.*

He heard Jonah leave a message for their father and then argue with Emma.

"Jonah, where's Dad?" William yelled over the rising wind.

"He didn't answer! I left a message," Jonah called up the ladder.

"Well, try the radio!" Jonah picked up the radio microphone, but there was no crackle. He flipped the switch on and off a few times.

"It's not working! I think the battery's dead!"

William zipped his lifejacket over his rain gear. He fought a rising panic. No captain wants to face a terrible storm without a battery. He took a deep breath. He had to keep calm for his brother and sister.

"The battery is probably fine. The storm just knocked out the radio. Call Dad every minute on the cell until he answers," William shouted above the wind. "Emma, come and help me navigate!"

Jonah called their father. Emma called out the degrees on the compass. William had to get the right heading to get them back to their harbour. There was no land, nothing to see or steer by, just dark water and darker clouds.

Then the storm hit.

Rain lashed their faces. Huge waves tossed them from side to side, soaking them. The wind howled and raged, and there was no sky, only clouds and darkness. The spray from the waves broke over the side of the boat, and the three sailors slipped and struggled, trying not to lose their footing.

There is nothing fun about being on a ship in a storm at sea. Stories are told about ship-wrecks and dangerous storms, which are great listening if you're warm and cozy and safely on land in front of a fireplace at home.

They are much less fun if you are actually *in one*.

And the Blackwells were in a *monster* of a storm.

William fought the wind, trying to keep *Peregrine* on course. Emma yelled out the compass headings.

Every minute, Jonah called their father. Suddenly, a huge crack of thunder and blaze of lightning flashed overhead, and then the cellphone didn't work.

No battery, no radio. And now, no cellphone.

"William! Start the motor!" Jonah yelled. William nodded. Why hadn't *he* thought of that? As he leaned down to start the motor, a huge wave smacked the ship sideways, and *Peregrine* flooded with water. The motor handle snapped off in William's hand.

Emma, Jonah, and William looked at each other. For a moment the good ship teetered, then righted.

No motor, either.

"The sea anchor!" William yelled. "Jonah, we're rolling! Grab the sea anchor!" Jonah scrambled to a locker. He tied a long line to the stern and the other end to a green bag and then tossed the bag overboard. The bag opened like a huge parachute, then sank below the waves.

It worked. As soon as the sea anchor hit the water, *Peregrine* stopped bucking and tossing. But a moment later, the next disaster!

RIPPPP!

With horror, the three sailors watched their foresail tear in half.

"The jib!" William yelled. The torn sail whipped madly back and forth, and *Peregrine* leaned hard over, closer and closer to the water.

"Jonah! Emma! Take the wheel together! I have to drop the sail! It's taking us over!"

"William! Leave it!" Emma yelled into the wind. She did NOT want William to run up to the front of the boat. But he was already half-way up the deck, crouched low, holding on to the handrail. The wind blew his hair in a mad dance, the water whipped into his face.

Emma could barely see him through the spray.

"William! Tie yourself to the lifeline!" she yelled. She saw him struggle with a line for a moment. Ahead of him, the torn sail flapped wildly. It tugged *Peregrine* closer and closer to the water. They could tip right over!

"Emma, help me!" Jonah yelled. Emma grabbed the wheel beside her brother and together they held the boat as steady as they could. The big steering wheel tossed them like rag dolls in the vicious wind. Wave after wave crashed over William, and water filled the cock-pit. Emma and Jonah were up to their ankles in water, trying hard not to slip. The scuppers gurgled with water. It sounded like drowning.

"We're sinking!" Emma cried.

"NO!" Jonah shouted. Emma peered through the streaming rain.

Where was William? An enormous wave crashed onto the deck ... and he was GONE!

"WILLIAM!" Emma screamed into the storm. For a second, Jonah and Emma looked at an empty deck.

Their brother was just washed *overboard*!

Emma and Jonah would talk about that moment for the rest of their lives. Storm, blackness, no motor, no radio, no cellphone, a ripped sail ... and their older brother washed away into the briny deep.

But at the time, in the teeth of the terrible storm, they did the only thing they could: they held on.

"WILLIAM! WILLIAM!" Emma screamed into the wind. With one hand, Jonah scooped the life-ring from its holder, ready to toss to William if he surfaced.

Then ... a hand appeared over the bow! And a second hand. Then William's head popped up over the front of the boat.

The lifeline had saved him!

William dragged himself onto the deck and collapsed in a gasping heap. A moment later, he reached up and dragged the torn sail down. He tied it tight, then slowly crawled back to the cockpit.

The three Blackwells stood together, clutching the wheel between them, as their sailboat bucked and danced in the waves.

The storm raged.

And still they sailed on.

CHAPTER FOUR

FINN

All storms eventually blow themselves out. As *Peregrine* sailed on and on, the winds slowly dropped. The waves fell.

The Blackwells were all asleep in the cockpit. Jonah lay on a bench. Emma lay on the cockpit floor. William was slumped over the wheel.

Peregrine and her sleeping crew drifted with the waves.

A thick, white fog rolled in. Soon the boat was a little island in the middle of a vast, silent ocean of fog. The cloud settled upon the water all around them.

The sailors were so still, anyone watching might think they were ... *enchanted*.

Suddenly a dolphin leapt near the boat. Or something that was *sort* of like a dolphin. Then a row of bubbles headed toward *Peregrine*. Two long, skinny hands grasped the railing, hands with slender fingers that dripped with seaweed.

A creature pulled itself onto the ship.

It was a *boy*. Or something boy-*like*, anyway.

He was tall and strong, but ribs showed below his ragged shirt. He wore old-fashioned pantaloons, torn at the knees. A shock of black hair tumbled across his face and shoulders, tangled with seaweed and starfish. In fact, seaweed wrapped around him, across his shoulders, down his arms. His feet and hands were long, much too long. Too long for his body.

He stepped into the cockpit and stood over the sleeping Blackwells.

A tattoo leapt along the boy's arm: *Finn*.

Finn crept first to William. He bent low and listened to the captain's slow breathing. Then Finn took something from his pocket — something green — and tucked it into William's mouth.

Finn crept next to Jonah, bent low, and listened. Again, Finn took something green from his pocket and tucked it onto Jonah's tongue. In his sleep, Jonah screwed up his eyes and mumbled, "Ew!"

But he didn't wake.

Then Finn reached out and gently moved Emma's hair out of her eyes. She stirred, so he plucked a piece of the green — whatever it was — and placed it on Emma's tongue. She screwed up her face but didn't wake. Then he reached behind his back and softly laid *something* beside her.

A gift.

Then lightning fast, he shimmied up the mast. At the top, he stared at *Peregrine*'s bright red ensign.

With a tug, he took it, and tied the red flag to his belt.

Then Finn, that strange boy from the sea — if he *was* a boy — dove from the mast, straight into the deep, black water below. Anyone watching, had anyone been awake, would have thought they saw a change in Finn as he hit the water.

They might have said he was more fish-like, certainly with hands and feet almost, well, like

fins. They might have watched in astonish-
ment as Finn surfaced and leapt into the air,
then back into the water.

Because they would have seen a dolphin.
Or something much like one, anyway.

But no one on board *Peregrine* saw a thing.
They slept and slept, while the thick fog rolled
around them.

And still *Peregrine* drifted on.

CHAPTER FIVE

SEAWEED AND FOGHORN

Emma opened her eyes first. The sound of the flapping main sail woke her. She lay face up in a pool of water in the cockpit.

She sat up.

Then she screwed up her face and pulled something out of her mouth.

EW! Seaweed? How did I get seaweed in my MOUTH?

The next second, Jonah sat up. And pulled seaweed from *his* mouth.

"Yuck! Seaweed?" He tossed the seaweed over the side of the boat.

Then William stirred and sat up. He

rubbed his eyes and shook his head. Then he screwed up his face and spat a piece of seaweed onto *his* palm.

He looked at it in wonder.

"What? How did that …?" He looked at his brother and sister. Amazed, he tossed the seaweed overboard.

The three of them stretched awake.

"Why is it so foggy?" Emma asked, looking around.

"And so still?" Jonah asked. They were right. The air was a thick, white cloud. It was eerie and quiet. They could only see the still, dark water right around the boat. There was nothing else but thick, muffled whiteness. There was no wind. Not a breath. Sailors call it "becalmed."

"Are you both all right?" William asked, standing up. The twins nodded.

"What's that?" Jonah pointed to something beside Emma. She stared at it then gently picked it up.

"A *conch shell*? But how did *that* get there?" She looked at her brothers, bewildered.

"How?" she demanded again. Jonah and William both looked surprised.

"It can't be yours, Emma," William finally said. "It just happens to be a shell that looks like it. Maybe it got washed in with a wave? It's strange, though. Maybe it's finally some good luck," he added.

"I'm putting it below," she said, then she climbed down into the cabin and examined the shell closely. It was *exactly* the same size and shape as her lost shell, but *how?*

There was no way to know if it *was* hers. Not for sure. But ... still.

She zipped the conch into her backpack. Something very strange was happening. She had almost decided it wasn't real, but it was hard to forget that long hand trailing seaweed, holding a shell above water. When did that happen exactly? It seemed like days ago, what with the weird burning phantom ship, the storm, and now the fog.

But her brothers didn't know about the hand. She should probably tell William ... but she doubted he'd believe her.

Who *would?*

Back on deck, the Blackwells surveyed the sailboat. *Peregrine* was a mess. Her foresail was torn, and there was a ragged halyard hanging from the mast. Lines and sheets were strewn across the deck. The line that held the sea anchor was torn.

"We lost our sea anchor," William said wearily.

"Our ensign is gone, too," Emma added. William and Jonah both looked up. She was right. Their bright red flag was missing from the top of the mast.

"It's never a good sign when a ship loses its ensign," Jonah said.

"Stop it, Jonah," William snapped. "No more talk of signs. The flag just blew away in the storm. We aren't sinking, we're all safe. Let's clean up *Peregrine*, then just try to get home."

"Where are we, anyway?" Jonah asked.

"I have no idea, and it's impossible to tell in the fog." William didn't want to say it, but they could be anywhere. He didn't know how long they'd slept, or where the storm had taken them.

They could be near land. Or they could be drifting out to sea....

"Jonah, can you keep track of the compass? Mark the time and the compass heading in the ship log every five minutes. We can see if we're drifting if we keep checking," William said. He rubbed his eyes. He was suddenly very tired, despite the sleep.

Is this how Dad feels after a storm, when he's captain? he wondered. He suddenly heard his father's voice: *A captain takes care of his crew first, William, then his ship.*

"Okay, Emma, Jonah, listen. It's been a strange trip. There's that weird burning ship, which we're not going to mention, then the storm, seaweed in our mouths, Emma's shell, now this fog. But we're okay. We're here. Dad will be looking for us. And I promise I'll get us home. But you both have to help."

"How are we going to get home? We're lost. We have no motor, no radio, no sails, no cellphone. We aren't going anywhere." Jonah peered into the thick cloud.

"The fog will lift eventually, and the wind will pick up again," William answered. "We'll paddle if we have to. Right now, let's eat and clean up *Peregrine*. And Emma, get the fog-horn going."

Emma groaned.

"Can't Jonah do it?" she asked. Some ships have air horns as foghorns, but their father believed in good old-fashioned breath. Their foghorn was heavy and made of brass. It was pretty to look at, maybe, but not very practical. She'd have to blow hard to make any noise at all. It was exhausting.

"Yes, you have to do it. Jonah is taking compass readings. You can switch in a while," William answered.

So, the Blackwells did what any crew does after a storm. They put aside whatever weird things had happened (because weird things do happen at sea during storms), and they took care of themselves and their ship.

William handed out apples, water, and crackers with cheese. They ate in silence. Then William tidied up lines, sheets, and the torn sail. Jonah took compass readings. And every three minutes, Emma took a huge breath and blew three blasts into the hated foghorn.

BUUUUUU! BUUUUUU! BUUUUUU!

If any other boats were out there, they'd know that *Peregrine* was near.

They drifted in the fog for a long while. The only sound was the foghorn or the occasional slap of water against the boat. In all that dull silence, it was hard not to fall back to sleep.

Then, just as Emma was about to blow into the foghorn again ...

"QUIET, EMMA! Listen!" William held his hand up to his ear.

CLANG. CLANG.

Suddenly a deep, low bell clanged! They all jumped to their feet.

"That's a buoy! A harbour marker!" William shouted.

"Yeah, but which one?" Jonah answered.

The bell clanged again as the sea gently rolled past it somewhere out in the fog. It was eerie hearing a low bell from an enormous harbour marker nearby. Not being able to see it made it doubly creepy. It could loom up at them at any second.

Anything could.

"It means we're near land!" William said.

He ran to the bow to listen. He concentrated and stared hard into the fog.

CLANG. CLANG. The bell was closer!

"It's coming from over there." Emma pointed.

CLANG. CLANG.

All three Blackwells leaned toward the sound ... suddenly the boat lurched.

CLUNK!

The boat lurched again, then it came to a full stop with a shudder. A loose plate rolled onto the cabin floor and broke. Everyone fell forward.

The Blackwells all peered hard into the fog.

"Is that … is that a *tree*?" Jonah whispered. A tree, then another tree and another, loomed out of the fog. It was eerie. What were trees doing off their bow?

"I think … I think we just ran aground," William said. But he was far less confident than he sounded.

What he didn't say?

But where are we? And what now?

CHAPTER SIX

THE DISTANT DRUMS

Peregrine was stuck.

"What did we hit?" Jonah ran to join his brother at the bow.

William lay flat on the deck and looked down at the water.

"It's sand! We hit a beach."

"Better than rocks," Jonah said.

William nodded. "Yes, little brother, definitely better than rocks. Hand me the boat hook and grab some paddles."

Jonah scurried down the ladder and came back up holding the long, curved boat hook and two paddles. He handed the boat hook to William, and a paddle to Emma.

William stabbed the boat hook down into the dark water. "It's not very deep, but *Peregrine* is really stuck. We're aground here until we get some wind again."

"But where are we?" Emma asked.

"We should take a vote," Jonah said. "Stay with the ship or go ashore and see where we are."

William shook his head. "No. We aren't staying with the boat. We might be on one of the islands near home. Or we might have crossed the bay in that storm and be near Dad. We could be anywhere. We have to go ashore and try to find out where we are." William slipped over the side into water up to his knees.

"It's not deep, and it's sandy," he said, heading to the beach. "Bring your paddles."

"Wait!" Emma ran into the cabin and grabbed her backpack with her inky mermaid. She wanted her mermaid with her, plus her shell. Somehow her shell came back to her, or *a* shell did, anyway, and it now seemed more precious than ever. She ran up the ladder, and as an afterthought, she grabbed the foghorn.

She slipped over the side of *Peregrine* into the shallow water. She ran to catch up with her brothers.

The three Blackwells walked on the shore. The beach was narrow between trees and water. William carried the boat hook and led the way along the foggy beach, Jonah behind him. Emma came up the rear with her paddle in one hand, the foghorn in the other. It took a few moments to get used to solid land again, even if it was sand. It put them all a little off balance.

"Um, William," Emma asked after a few steps.

"Yeah?"

"Do those trees look *normal* to you?"

William stopped. "What do you mean …?" But the words died on his lips. Emma was right. There *was* something a little wrong about the trees.

"Why are they *palm trees*?" Jonah added. William hadn't noticed. He was so happy to find land, he hadn't actually *looked* at it.

William considered the trees. "Yes, I agree that's a little odd. Why would there be palm trees?" He sounded calm. Too calm. There WAS no explanation for the jungle of palm trees crowding the beach. There was a whole continent, not to mention an ocean, between their home and the nearest palm trees. He blinked. He swallowed. He tried to clear his mind.

"Let's not think too much about the trees, please." Emma and Jonah looked at their older brother, but they were both too brave, or possibly too worried, to ask any more questions about why there would be palm trees.

"How will we find the ship again?" Jonah asked. They had only taken a few steps, and *Peregrine* was already almost hidden in the fog behind them.

"We'll mark a trail as we go," William said. He dragged his foot along the beach and made a large arrow in the sand, pointing back toward *Peregrine*.

William was acting too calm. And a little grim.

"We'll see these arrows plus our footprints in the sand. And I'll blaze a trail on the trees. Come on, let's go." Emma had a sinking feeling as she looked behind her and saw *Peregrine* fade in the fog.

She gripped the paddle and the foghorn a little harder.

When he counted fifty steps, William took his army knife and slashed an arrow on one of the palm trees along the shore. It pointed back toward *Peregrine*. Or where they all hoped *Peregrine* waited in the fog.

The island was quiet. The harbour marker had stopped clanging — everything was so still.

And it was weirdly hot. It was summer, but this was different. Almost a tropical heat. They were too hot even in T-shirts. They walked quietly along the beach for a few minutes. Then they reached a wall of boulders. They couldn't go any farther along the beach.

A sandy pathway led into the trees.

William stopped suddenly and held up a hand for quiet.

BOOM BOOM da-dum!

BOOM BOOM da-dum!

William looked at Emma and Jonah. Jonah's eyes were huge. Emma clutched the foghorn and the paddle.

The sound came again.

BOOM BOOM da-dum!

BOOM BOOM da-dum!

"What is it?" Emma whispered. William shook his head and put his fingers to his lips, listening hard. It came once more.

BOOM BOOM da-dum!
BOOM BOOM da-dum!

"I'm not sure, but I think it's … *drums*. Far away, though."

"Drums? Why drums?" Emma asked. The place was weirding her out. She didn't want to look too closely, but she was pretty sure she just saw a *parrot* flitting in the palm trees.

That can't be a parrot. That's a tropical bird, she said to herself. *You're seeing things.*

William dropped his voice to a whisper. "Jonah, run down the pathway into the trees, fifty steps, look around, then come right back."

Jonah looked a little worried. "Why me?"

"Okay, I'll go, you stay here with Emma," William said.

"No! Don't leave me with Jonah," Emma begged. William shot his little brother a "*see?*" look. Jonah swallowed.

BOOM BOOM da-dum!
BOOM BOOM da-dum!

"Can I have the boat hook?" Jonah asked. William swapped the boat hook for Jonah's paddle. Emma had never seen her twin looked so scared.

The drums were probably nothing, right? A drumming group practising.

In the middle of nowhere. In the fog.

On a weirdly tropical and lonely beach.

"William, maybe we should stick together?" she said.

But William shook his head. "No, I want two of us to stay on the beach to keep near *Peregrine*. Besides, Jonah is the fastest runner. Just run into the trees, take a look, then run right back." Emma was about to argue that they could all run into the trees and back together, but Jonah interrupted her.

"Okay, wish me luck," he said. Emma could see he didn't want to do it ... but she also knew he didn't want to seem scared. So she and William stood on the beach and watched Jonah disappear into the dark, strange palm trees.

"You don't have to go far, just let us know if the pathway keeps going," William called after him.

Jonah jogged onto the pathway. It was dark as soon as he left the beach. The palm trees blocked the light, what there was of it in the fog, almost right away. He counted as he ran: one, two, three steps. He kept going until he hit twenty-three steps.

What was that?

Something moved in the trees to his right. Something fast.

Jonah stopped. His heart hammered. He gulped and gripped the boat hook with both hands.

Something whipped past him again, just out of sight. He held his breath. He gripped the boat hook tighter. He turned to run back toward the beach …

… but a huge, dark figure stepped onto the pathway.

Jonah's shriek filled the air.

When William and Emma reached the spot a minute later, the boat hook lay on the ground.

Jonah was gone!

CHAPTER SEVEN

MIGHT THEY BE MERMAIDS?

"Jonah!" Emma shouted into the dark trees.

"SHH!" William clapped his hand over her mouth. He shook his head and put his finger to his lips. If William were alone, he probably wouldn't have been acting so calm.

But he wasn't alone. He had his little sister with him. And he was trying hard not to scare her. Or show her how scared he was. Her eyes were huge, and she clutched the paddle and foghorn with white knuckles.

Where was Jonah? Why had he dropped the boat hook?

I shouldn't have split us up, William thought. *Emma was right. Or maybe we should have stayed with the boat until the fog cleared and the wind picked up, like Jonah wanted.*

He had to decide what to do.

It's possible that Jonah just went to … pee? Or maybe he's hiding and trying to scare us? He'd think it was hilarious.

But what about the shriek?

I really wish Dad was here.

"William, do you hear singing?" Emma whispered.

William strained to listen. The sun peeked through the trees. The fog was lifting.

And yes, there *was* a song on the breeze.

But a strange one. A weird, shrieking, high-pitched sound, if you could call *that* singing.

"I hear something, but I can't imagine what's singing with a voice like that," he whispered. *And I'm not sure I want to find out.*

A bizarre and watery song filled the air. It sounded like water bubbles popping while someone shrieked.

"Let's go find who's singing. Maybe they know where Jonah is," Emma whispered.

William looked down at his little sister. What choice did they have? "Okay, stay close," he said quietly. He carried a paddle in one hand and the boat hook in the other. Together, the two remaining Blackwells walked quietly along the sandy pathway, deeper into the palm trees. They followed the strange singing.

It got louder.

They weaved through the trees. Shafts of sunlight fell to the sandy pathway; the fog had lifted now. And still they walked on.

The singing got louder.

Suddenly, the trees stopped.

The singing stopped, too.

William and Emma stepped onto a sandy beach that overlooked a shallow lagoon. Rocks broke the surface of the water, which rippled like a living thing. Emma ran down to the water, and William followed. There was something odd about the water, though. It rippled and moved, and suddenly William saw what lay just beneath the surface.

"Wait, Emma!"

With a burbling yell, bodies rose from the water all around them!

Emma froze. An army of terrifying creatures filled the lagoon. Hundreds of scaly, green faces and wet, black eyes stared at her. Long, green seaweed-hair waved, and upturned teeth jutted from wet, bulging lips. The horrifying creatures shook shark jawbones and pointed at Emma with spiny, wicked fingers.

Emma dropped her paddle and screamed. William grabbed her hand and turned to run back across the beach …

… but the army of ferocious mermaids (for what else could they be?) threw their swampy nets.

William fell! A seaweed net covered his head and shoulders. A sea-kelp rope snared his legs, then shark jawbone spears fell along the beach. The kelp rope dragged him — tug by tug — toward the watery horde. Each fishy mouth opened, and horrible shrieking screams filled the air. Emma stared in shock.

"Run, Emma! Run back to the boat!" William yelled. Emma jumped and tried to pull the net off her brother, but it was no use. The net clung like barnacles (in fact, the merfolk used barnacle juice for that very reason), and the rope held like steel.

The mermaid mob crowded the shallow water, crawling onto the beach, slapping their tails in the unfamiliar air. They dragged William through the sand toward them, netted like a giant land fish.

"RUN, EMMA! RUN!" William screamed, just before the writhing mermaids dragged him into the water and fell upon him.

Emma turned and fled along the pathway, back into the sheltering trees.

CHAPTER EIGHT

ZOMBIE PIRATES FROM THE BRINY DEEP

"**B**oil his bones! Shiver me timbers!"

"The queen will want to speak with him!"

"You great, lumbering fool!"

Jonah heard angry voices. He couldn't remember much after *something* big had grabbed him on the pathway in the trees. Huge, bony hands had covered his eyes with a blindfold, stuck him in a sack, then dumped him here, wherever this was.

His whole body hurt, and he had a terrible headache. Plus he was thirsty.

And cramped. He sat in a box with his arms tied behind his back. He slowly opened his eyes and realized he was sitting in a wooden cage. Light shone through the wooden bars, and he could dimly see two enormous people, or two enormous *somethings* anyway, moving around.

They were yelling at each other.

"But what if he's a friend of hers?" said a man's voice.

"Well, he's *ours* now!" said a woman.

"But we should tell her!"

"And why would we want to do that?"

"For the ..." the man dropped his voice to a theatrical, loud whisper, "... *curse*. You havn't forgotten about *that*, have you?"

The room rocked gently, and Jonah could hear sails flap in the wind. *I'm on a sailboat,* he thought. *But WHAT sailboat?*

"But who is he?"

The man said, "How should I know? He's probably hers, and she'll pay handsome to get him back. We should bang the drums again, let her know we got one of hers."

The woman tut-tutted. "Yer a fool, brother. Think on it. If he IS hers, she'll be awful angry with us for taking him. If he ISN'T hers, she'll be awful angry with us for bothering her."

"Naw, sister, we say we saved him from ..."

"From what?"

"From … pirates?"

Jonah heard a scuffle and a clunk, like someone hit something heavy.

"*We're* the pirates!" There was more scuffling and shoving.

"He's awful skinny," the woman said.

"Not much meat on him," the man said.

"I'm not even sure he IS one of the merfolk." The woman again.

"Well, he sure ain't a pirate," added the man.

Then a third voice, more of a squawk than anything else, said, "Pieces of eight! Boil his bones! Shiver me timbers!"

A parrot? Jonah wondered. *Where am I?*

Then there was some whispering that Jonah didn't like the sound of at all. He definitely heard the man's voice say, "gut him and throw him overboard," and the woman added, "not enough to cook."

Cook?

Jonah swallowed hard. Then shouted, "I'm not for cooking! And I don't belong to anyone!"

The whispering stopped.

"And … and I'm not one of the merfolk. Or a pirate. I'm a *boy*. My name is Jonah."

The top of the box opened.

Two terrible faces stared at him.

Jonah tried not to scream.

Two skulls stared down. With long, stringy hair and staring eyes and fleshless grins. Jonah saw rotted flesh where skin should be, ripped clothes, tattered bandanas....

This can't be real!

Jonah closed his eyes. And opened them again.

The skulls still grinned down at him. They didn't smell terribly sweet, either, since the two … whatevers … looked like they hadn't bathed. Ever. A huge, bony hand reached into the box and hauled Jonah to his feet.

Jonah was plunked down in front of the two … *pirates?*

For they could only be pirates. Right down to the one with the gold tooth and the one with an eye-patch.

Correction, Jonah thought. *Two ZOMBIE pirates. Cursed ones. With skulls, don't forget about the skulls.*

They appeared to be long dead.

Jonah swallowed. He was right about the parrot, though. There was a bright green parrot, on a perch in the middle of the cabin. It stared at him then opened and closed its beak. It, at least, appeared not to be a zombie. It sat beside a pile of coconuts and bananas.

"Jonah?" the brother zombie pirate demanded. This was Gold-Tooth. Jonah nodded. Now that he was standing in front of them, Jonah realized how tall they were. Enormous. They were doubled over in the low cabin.

"What's a 'boy'?" the sister pirate asked. This was Eye-Patch. Jonah gulped.

"You don't know what a *boy* is?" he asked, backing toward the ladder. The sun shone brightly up on deck. Wherever Jonah was, the fog had lifted.

"Shiver me timbers! Pieces of eight!" the parrot shrieked.

"No. My sister and I haven't had the pleasure …" Gold-Tooth said, advancing on him.

"You're not one of them slippery *kaboutermannekes*, are you?" Eye-Patch asked, moving beside her brother.

"A kab … ooter … a *what*?" Jonah slowly backed up toward the ladder. The pirates advanced, just as slowly. There was a very fierce, strange look about them. Like they hadn't eaten in a while. Eye-Patch slowly smiled.

If it *was* a smile. Without lips, a smile isn't really a smile. It's a dark, scary grimace.

"Aw, listen, the whelp don't know about the sea spirits." The pirates started to laugh (just imagine what *that* sounded like), and Jonah saw his chance. He grabbed a coconut and threw it.

Bonk!

He hit Gold-Tooth right between the eyes! All those years of baseball practice paid off! Then Jonah scampered up the ladder. Bony hands grabbed his ankles, but he kicked and climbed, kicked and climbed.

Click! Jonah's foot connected and something heavy landed on the cabin floor. Whatever it was, it rolled around.

"Where's my head!" Eye-Patch called.

Jonah DID NOT want to look down and see zombie pirates on their hands and knees, searching frantically for a lost head. He ran onto the deck of the ship.

And WHAT a ship! A gigantic set of black drums sat beside the wheel. Black sails, black deck, a huge black mast flew a black flag with a grinning white skull on it.

The Jolly Roger! The pirate's ensign!

Jonah *was* stuck on a pirate ship.

Correction! Zombie pirate ship!

And two angry, cursed pirates — one possibly headless — were running up the ladder after him!

CHAPTER NINE

THE MERMAID QUEEN

William looked over the water. The blazing sun shone down.

He was hot. He was thirsty.

He was tied to a rock in the middle of the lagoon.

His shirt and shorts were ripped. William was tattered and torn.

The boat hook and the paddles from *Peregrine* were stuck into the rock at his feet. The water rippled, and strange seaweed hair and dark green fins broke the still surface. All around him, the mermaid army lurked just below the water, guarding him.

Where do they think I'd possibly be going? he wondered grimly.

He could see their green faces and scaly arms below the water.

And fins.

He shuddered.

I hope Jonah and Emma are okay, he thought. *I'm still their captain. I have to get out of this and get us home.*

The thought of finding his little brother and sister was the only thing that kept him calm.

All through his ordeal, William tried hard not to look too closely at the creatures holding him captive on the rock. He tried not to think about the weird phantom ship, or the storm, or the fog, or anything that had happened during his short, disastrous term as captain of *Peregrine*.

I'm likely unconscious, still on the deck of Peregrine, he thought, again and again.

I probably got hit by the boom during the storm. I'm hallucinating, or really sick or something. Isn't this when the hero arrives? Who's the hero of this story, I wonder? It sure isn't me!

William stood on the rock. The sun beat down. He wanted a drink of water. He wanted to wipe the sweat from his face. He thought about maidens left out for dragons in movies about knights. He thought about sailors dying of thirst on desert islands. He thought about every mermaid movie he'd ever seen and how wrong the world was about mermaids.

Just as William was slipping into a weird, dazed dream …

… the water stirred at his feet.

The army of seaweed-strewn heads stirred and broke the surface of the lagoon. A strong ripple started then grew to a small wave, then a much bigger wave. There were tiny, fierce sharks in the wave, all teeth and jaws, snapping at the mermaids in the water.

The creatures guarding him silently moved aside. A large fish — oh, how he wished it were a fish, but somehow he knew it wasn't — swam through the throng toward him. A crown of whalebone rode above the waves, followed by a long, silver fin churning the green and foamy wake.

William swallowed. He took a deep breath.

Whatever was coming for him … it was coming *now*.

William stood to face whatever it was.

An enormous wave grew and boiled at his feet. The stench of rotten fish filled the air, and the wave was brimming with larger sharks and cascading crabs and spiny starfish, falling like a fountain and rising up again into the wave.

From the middle of the fountain, *she* rose. A huge bony skull with upturned teeth and seaweed for hair. The whalebone crown topped the slimy face, and long, scaly arms clutched a whalebone sword.

Black eyes rolled in sockets above a fishy mouth.

The monster rose above William, the giant wave roiling faster and faster, cascading sharks and crabs into the deep. The long, silver fin that ran down the monster's back was lost in the depths.

A horrifying burbling sound, like the scream of a thousand drowned sailors, rasped a question: "WHO DARES TO DISTURB THE MERMAID QUEEN?"

William stared. But he didn't scream.

He looked up into the face of the horror before him and had only one thought: *If I'm dreaming, isn't this when I should wake up?*

CHAPTER TEN

THE FIGUREHEAD GRAVEYARD

Emma tore along the pathway. She ran through the trees and kept running. Finally, she fell onto the sand, where it was very dark and still.

She was as far from the beach, and those monster mermaids, as she could get!

I have to help William! And find Jonah! If I find Peregrine, maybe the radio will be working now that the storm is over, and I can call Dad. Or someone. I am definitely NOT going back to the lagoon! I hope William is okay!

Emma had to decide what to do, fast. She had lost her paddle on the beach, but she still had the foghorn. And her backpack. And her conch shell. Or *a* conch shell. Just knowing it was in her backpack made her feel better somehow.

Okay, just find Peregrine. *Maybe Jonah's there, too, and we can save William together!*

Emma ran along the pathway. If she could find the beach, she might see one of William's marks on a tree. Or his arrows or their footprints in the sand. All of those could lead her back to the sailboat.

She ran quietly across the warm sand.

And stopped.

Something moved in the trees ahead of her.

It moved again.

It can't be one of those mermaid things — we're nowhere near the water. Unless they can walk on land.

Emma shuddered at the thought. She ducked behind a tree.

Then something moved again, lightning fast, and ran past her, shoving her to the ground. She sat up in time to see a boy run away down the path.

A very tall, thin boy in old-fashioned, ragged clothes. At least, it *might* be a boy. She was about to run in the opposite direction when something caught her eye.

The boy had dropped something red in the sandy pathway.

Emma took a few steps forward. She poked the red thing with her toe.

It was a flag. *And it had a white and grey bird on it!*

Peregrine's ensign!

She picked it up, astonished. It *was* their lost flag! But what was *that* doing here? She studied it a moment longer and then tied it to her backpack.

What did it mean? She stared after the boy. Behind her was the terrible mermaid lagoon. Ahead of her was a boy who somehow had *Peregrine*'s flag. Maybe he could help?

Emma started after the boy, very cautiously, peering through the trees. She could have sworn she saw a monkey scamper up a tree. But when she looked carefully … nothing was there. The boy's footprints in the sand were strange, as though he had giant, floppy feet. His prints veered off into the trees.

"Hello?" she called, quietly. The trees grew farther apart. She walked through them and stopped. She stood in a clearing. Bright sunshine shone down onto a large, grassy circle.

Emma stared. All around the circle, strange, wooden statues stood in the grass. Emma took a few steps closer. The statues were as tall as she was or much taller.

And they were the strangest statues she'd ever seen.

The first wooden statue was a soldier.

A very *ancient* soldier.

"A *gladiator*?" she whispered. It was definitely a Roman gladiator, with a short sword and a soldier's helmet. He was faded, and some of his nose was worn away, and most of his silver paint was chipped off. But Emma had seen pictures of gladiators like him at school when she studied Roman times. He towered over her, glaring with blank, wooden eyes.

It was a little creepy.

She walked slowly past the gladiator and studied the next wooden statue. This was a lady with spectacles, wearing an old-fashioned bonnet and long dress. The woman clutched a book. She was faded and worn, too. But Emma could see that her long, flowing, black skirt must have looked wonderful when it was freshly painted.

Whenever that was. The wooden statues were old — very old — hundreds of years old, probably.

Emma walked past more statues. Here was a very young girl with flowers in her hair, wearing a long dress. And there an English knight with a broken lance and a sword. Next to him was a galloping horse with a flowing mane and front legs pounding through sea foam. Then a sea captain with a pipe, a hat, and a jacket with large buttons. Next, a carved wooden monkey held coconuts. Beside the monkey, a giant, coiled snake curled upon itself. Next to them, a faded mermaid sat on a rock, one hand playing in her hair. Emma moved closer.

Now this was what a mermaid was *supposed* to look like. Not scaly and terrifying. Although this one was definitely a little sad, Emma had to admit.

Emma walked slowly around the ring and counted ten wooden statues in all. Something about the way the statues were stuck in the ground and how old they were seemed familiar.

I know what this reminds me of, she thought with a shudder. *This looks like an old graveyard! Except they're statues with faces instead of gravestones.*

She walked to the last statue.

This wooden statue was a dolphin leaping out of the water. The dolphin looked so

joyful, so alive, that Emma drew in close. Not *quite* a dolphin.

The dolphin's eyes were starfish. And the dolphin's fins were not quite right, more hands and feet than fins.

And the dolphin … was *wet*!

One of the starfish eyes winked at her.

"Ah-ha, you've found me!" the dolphin said.

Emma dropped the foghorn. She was about to turn and run when the dolphin twisted and changed into someone she had seen before.

The boy!

"Welcome to the figurehead graveyard, Emma," he said. He was tall and thin and wore torn, tattered clothes. But he was definitely … a boy. Or boy-*like*, anyway.

"Wh-what?" she stammered. She backed away.

"Not what. *Who*," the boy said with a mischievous smile. Emma noticed a tattoo along his arm: *Finn*.

"W-w-who?" Emma stared at him. She was afraid to turn her head, because she *did not* like the glimpses of movement she saw out of the corner of her eye.

She did *not like them AT ALL*.

"I'm Finn." He grinned at her.

"F-F-Finn?" Emma stammered. She kept her back firmly turned to the other statues. Now was *not* the time to fall apart. Or ask too many questions. She wasn't sure she wanted to hear the answers.

And what's a figurehead graveyard? she wondered. Figureheads were the carvings on the bow of old ships, like the phantom ship they'd seen. That one had a screaming mermaid on it. *The Mermaid Queen*, it was called.

"It's all right, really," Finn said, gently. He picked up her foghorn. "We've met before, although you were asleep. I took your ensign," he said, pointing at the flag tied to her backpack. "I put seaweed in your mouth, too. And in your brother's mouths. After the storm."

Emma stared at him. She refused to pay attention to the movements flickering behind her. *I'm sleeping. I'm aboard* Peregrine, *still asleep in the fog. This can't be real.*

"Seaweed? In my mouth? Why?" She held his gaze, but there were soft noises behind her, now. Strange rustlings …

"To save you, of course," Finn said. "You and your brothers were drowning. I'm sure this seems very strange."

Emma stared at him for a moment. Then …

… "*Strange?* STRANGE! I just saw *ter-rifying mermaids* capture my brother, and I have no idea where my other brother is! STRANGE! YOU just turned from a *dolphin* into a *boy* before my eyes! STRANGE? YES! I'd say it's all pretty strange, wouldn't you! And drowning? What do you mean, *drowning?*" A small part of her was thinking, *Shouting is much better than screaming. A little better, anyway. At least I'm still making sense.*

The movements behind her were suddenly bigger, harder to ignore. They were accompanied by occasional swishings.

And stampings. And the *clank* of metal.

Emma swallowed and slowly turned around.

The Roman gladiator stood right behind her. His silver helmet glistened in the sun. He wasn't faded, and his nose wasn't broken anymore. He blinked then bowed slightly.

Beside him stood the English knight in full metal armour. His sword looked very sharp.

The schoolteacher with the spectacles and the book stood beside him. Her long black skirt blew in the gentle breeze. She held the hand of the little girl with the flowers in her hair.

Next to them the sea captain stood, his pipe smoke curling gently up into the sunlit afternoon.

Nearby, the horse swished its tail and chomped the grass while the monkey chattered down at them from a tree. The sad mermaid looked at them, but she hadn't moved from her spot. The giant snake was nowhere to be seen.

The wooden statues weren't wooden anymore.

They were *alive*.

And they all looked at Emma with concern.

"Are you all right, milady?" the knight asked in a very English accent. He leaned gently toward her. And that, *that* was the moment that Emma's knees gave out, and she finally fell in the grass and closed her eyes.

Because *none* of this could really be happening.

Could it?

CHAPTER ELEVEN

GOLD-TOOTH AND EYE-PATCH

Jonah stood on the gang-plank, his hands tied behind him. The hot sun shone down. The waves slapped the pirate ship below him.

He squinted at the pirates, who were arguing. Again. For brother and sister, they didn't get along very well.

"But what if he DOES belong to the queen?" Gold-Tooth said.

"Well then, he can swim, can't he?" Eye-Patch answered.

"I'm NOT with the queen. I keep telling you that," Jonah shouted at them for the thousandth time.

Now, Jonah wasn't sure why the pirates were so angry. Although kicking off one of their zombie skull heads certainly hadn't helped. And playing hide-and-seek with them all across their ship probably hadn't helped either.

In the end, Jonah had run up the mast.

But that's where they caught him, since once you go up the mast, eventually you have to come down. Eye-Patch climbed up after him, and that was the end of the running away part of the day.

Then the pirates had tied him up again, and here he was, walking the gang-plank.

"To the queen!" Gold-Tooth said again.

"To the bottom of the ocean!" Eye-Patch yelled.

"Boil his bones! Shiver me timbers!" the green parrot called. It flew in circles over their heads.

Jonah rolled his eyes. He'd had enough. "Look, let's get on with this, can we! I'm tired of listening to you two fight. I say let's go see this queen. Why not? She'll tell you I'm not one of hers."

Now, these two pirates were not what you'd call terribly *bright*. Surely there must be some smart pirates somewhere. But this quarrelling brother and sister definitely weren't them.

Jonah was beginning to realize that his appearance was the most exciting and confusing thing that had ever happened to them.

The pirates stared at him.

"What did you say?" Gold-Tooth demanded.

"Well, I just said, let's get this over with and go and see the queen. You two can't seem to decide what to do with me. Why not let her decide?"

Gold-Tooth drew up close to Jonah and pulled out his sword. It was awfully sharp and glinted in the sun. He put it against Jonah's back. Jonah flinched and took another step toward the end of the gang-plank.

"Why should we take you to the Mermaid Queen?"

Mermaid Queen?

"Well, maybe she can help you."

Both pirates blinked at Jonah.

"Help us?" Gold-Tooth asked, confounded.

"Well, yes! With the curse you keep talking about. The one that's made you … like you are," Jonah spluttered. He couldn't bring himself to say "into zombies."

He was starting to feel light-headed. This was all just too weird. The hot sun, the zombie pirates, the shrieking parrot. Where was William? Where was Emma? It was possible that this was all a weird dream and he was still asleep on the deck of *Peregrine*, in the fog.

But at the thought of Emma, Jonah felt a tiny pang of guilt. The pirates' quarrelling was suddenly a little too familiar.

"But she's the one who made us INTO zombies!" Gold-Tooth growled and jabbed his sword at Jonah again. "And she DON'T want to be disturbed for a water rat like you!"

"But I'm not a water rat!" Jonah yelled. "I can sail! I can help you sail this ship. One of you can be the captain and the other the first mate. I'll be the cabin boy!"

The pirates grew suddenly quiet. Jonah strained to see what was happening behind him. The pirates eyed each other and slowly began to circle the deck, swords drawn.

"But I'm the captain, sister!" Gold-Tooth hissed.

"Beggar your bones, I'm the captain, *little* brother!" snarled Eye-Patch.

"No, I'm the captain!" yelled Jonah, pretending to be one of the pirates. The pirates circled each other, growling. He had hit on the very thing to infuriate them. He knew *exactly* how to stir up a brother and sister, it seemed. There was that little pang of guilt, again.

"No, I AM!" shouted Gold-Tooth.

"Over my headless corpse! I'm older!" shouted Eye-Patch.

"I told you, I'm the captain," Jonah shouted again, just to keep things going.

Clang! Clang!

The pirates crossed swords, forgetting all about Jonah. He saw his chance! He rolled off the gang-plank and ran to the wheel.

The brother and sister circled the deck, their swords pointed at each other.

"I tell you, I'M the CAPTAIN of this ship!" That was Eye-Patch.

"I'll boil you alive in hot tar before I let YOU be the CAPTAIN! You're the first mate, that's good enough for you!" That was Gold-Tooth.

Clang! Clang!

"I'll skewer you through and through before I see *you* be CAPTAIN!" yelled a third voice, which sounded a lot like Jonah.

The pirates circled each other, back and forth across the deck, closer and closer to the sides. Jonah wriggled his hands free of their ties and crouched behind the wheel.

Just a little closer, go just a little closer.

"I tell you this, sister, YOU WILL NEVER BE CAPTAIN OF THIS SHIP!" Gold-Tooth held Eye-Patch at the edge of the deck with the point of his sword.

"And neither will you!" yelled Jonah. And with that, Jonah turned the wheel with all his strength. The ship lurched hard. Both pirates looked astonished, just before they lost their balance and fell overboard!

SPLASH! SPLASH!

Jonah steered the pirate ship toward the island. He ignored the zombie pirates calling him names from the water — what exactly was a "sea dog" anyway? — and kept his eye on the horizon.

He had a pirate ship to sail. And his brother and sister to find!

CHAPTER TWELVE

IT'S SUNDOWN SOMEWHERE

The water rose and rose around William.

A huge wall of foam burst from the ocean, and waves rolled upon themselves, high above his head. Sea creatures, small fish, crabs, sea horses, and less pleasant sharks, barracuda, and ancient horseshoe crabs, swirled in the water, rising and falling into the ocean, only to rise again.

Sea foam doused him. He tried not to splutter, and he kept his head up; looking at the sea monster before him.

The Mermaid Queen held the whalebone sword in one spiny hand. She reached forward and plucked *Peregrine*'s boat hook from the rock and shook it at William with the other. Two large mermaids each held one of *Peregrine*'s paddles and stood guard beside him. The rest of the mermaid army rose above the water, too. A thousand seaweed-swept heads gnashed horrible teeth and shook fish-bone weapons at William.

The Mermaid Queen looked drowned, a thousand years dead. Seaweed hair swept from her fierce forehead, and her silver lips were swollen, bitten by her ferocious mouth of teeth, row upon row, behind them.

William stood in shock. This creature was *nothing* like Emma's mermaids. *Nothing.*

I will never let Jonah tease Emma about mermaids again if I get out of this, he thought.

The Mermaid Queen stared down at William tied to the rock and spoke in her terrible drowned voice. "WHO ARE YOU?"

"I'm … I'm William Blackwell, older brother to Emma and Jonah Blackwell and captain of the good ship *Peregrine,*" he croaked. *I sound completely crazy,* he thought. *And why am I talking like I'm from the 1800s?*

The Mermaid Queen's eyes were huge, black, wet. When she blinked they rolled backward and turned white like a shark's.

"CAPTAIN?" the queen roared, blowing water across William in a slimy gush. All the mermaids in the lagoon howled, enraged. Clearly, they didn't like captains.

William nodded. "Y-yesss." *Although not a great one, it seems*, he thought.

This cannot be real. I can't actually be standing here talking to the Mermaid Queen. Who ever heard of a Mermaid Queen? I'm really still stuck in the fog, sleeping on Peregrine. *I hope. It's about time I woke up, though ...*

"DOES THIS WEAKLING LUNG-BREATHER KNOW WHAT WE DO TO CAPTAINS?" the queen shrieked, and all the mermaids in the lagoon cheered. They knew.

The queen drew her horrible, dead-fish face close to William. The stench of rotten fish and decayed sea-life almost knocked him over. He *might* have fallen over, had he not been tied to the rock. Seagulls screamed and cried far above.

William tried his best to look at her. It wasn't easy. He closed one eye and tilted his head.

"*WE DROWN THEM*," she hissed, water burbling through her lips. Then a frill of fins rose around her head in a horrible fan and she shook them at William, while her mermaid army slapped the water and shrieked. He closed his eyes.

I'm unconscious. I'm dreaming. I'm on board Peregrine. *This is all just a weird nightmare.*

"DO YOU KNOW *WHEN* WE DROWN THEM?" she cried. William shook his head.

"WE DROWN THEM AT *SUNDOWN*!" She pointed the boat hook to the horizon. The sun was still a few hours from sinking. Sundown?

Then all the mermaids slapped the water and shrieked, and the noise was a terrifying wave that broke upon the prisoner on the rock.

The mermaids began to swim in tight circles around him, and the water rose and rose.

The churning water slowly rose to William's knees. Then to his waist. Then to his chest. It rose to just below his chin and stayed there as the legion of sea-dwellers swam around and around him in dizzying circles.

The Mermaid Queen sat behind them, gnashing her rows of teeth.

The water crested just below William's nose.

The mermaids parted, and the queen came forth.

"IT'S SUNDOWN SOMEWHERE ON THE BRINY DEEP! MAYBE WE SHOULD DROWN YOU NOW!" She thrust the whalebone sword at William's head, and he ducked below the water.

He came up spluttering.

"ANY LAST WORDS BEFORE YOU DIE, CAPTAIN WILLIAM BLACKWELL OF THE GOOD SHIP *PEREGRINE*?" William stared at her, his heart pounding, his teeth chattering. *My little brother and sister deserve better than me as a captain*, he thought.

But … I'm all they have!

"What words would I have for you? I've done nothing to you!" William shouted, blowing water from his lips. "I don't even know why I'm here or what you want with me! I just want to find my ship, gather my brother and sister, and go home! I AM the captain of *Peregrine*, and there's nothing you can do to change that!"

William was suddenly angry. For a dream or a hallucination or whatever this was, the Mermaid Queen was awfully real. Not to mention that his head was about to slip forever below the waves.

Someone please wake me up!

He was a captain without a ship or a crew. He was a sailor lost at sea, about to drown, like so many had drowned before him. A tiny flicker of white-hot anger started in his chest. He didn't have time for this, whatever this was. He had to find Emma and Jonah!

"I'll get my crew home AND save my ship! That's what captains do!" he yelled.

The Mermaid Queen let out a shriek. She laid the heavy whale bone sword on top of his head and with one quick push shoved William below the water.

He gulped one final breath and sank below the waves.

CHAPTER THIRTEEN

THE MERMAID CURSE

Emma opened her eyes.

Nearby, the horse chomped the long grass and lazily flicked its tail in the shade. The monkey chattered from a tree. The sad mermaid played with her hair, still in her spot.

But above Emma, a circle of concerned faces looked down at her in the grass. A medieval knight in armour. A Roman gladiator. A schoolteacher. A little girl with a daisy-chain of flowers in her hair. A sea captain. And Finn.

The coiled snake was nowhere to be seen.

Emma closed her eyes again for a moment. She took a deep breath.

I'm probably still on Peregrine, *asleep, and this is all a weird dream. It doesn't matter if this is real or not. Just find William and Jonah!*

Emma sat up. Finn offered his hand, and she shakily took it. He pulled her to her feet.

"It's all right, lass," the sea captain said. He took a few puffs of his pipe.

"*Sumus amici,*" said the gladiator.

"He only speaks Latin," the schoolteacher added matter-of-factly.

Of course he only speaks Latin, Emma thought. *Why not?* She crossed her arms. She frowned. It would be *very easy* to let her brain wander. For one thing, where exactly WAS that giant snake, anyway?

"But he said, 'We are friends,'" the little girl said, proudly.

"Well done, Mary-Celeste." The schoolteacher beamed, patting the little girl on the shoulder.

Finn stepped forward. "The shipwrecked figureheads need your help, Emma," he said.

"Shipwrecked? Figureheads?"

"Yes. Each of these figureheads belonged to ships wrecked here long ago, lured by the mermaids. Their queen cursed them to stay here upon this island as her prisoner in this graveyard." Finn looked over his shoulder at the sad mermaid and dropped his voice.

"Our mermaid was the first. And she's SO cursed, she can't even move. She's the *wrong* kind of mermaid, apparently."

"But you come and go," Emma pointed out.

"I'm not cursed," he said quietly. "I choose to be here. But we're all sea spirits ... or some say *kaboutermannekes*."

Emma shook her head.

"Pardon?"

"Ka-bout-er-mann-e-kes," Finn said. Emma just looked at him.

"We're ancient, wandering sea spirits, Emma. We swim the seas, save the drowning, or lead lost sailors to safety. You'll find us in many forms, in figureheads, even in dolphins. I was never shipwrecked, I was not cursed, so I'm free to come and go, but they're not." He nodded at the other figureheads. "All they want is to be free to return to the sea, like me."

Emma took a quick look at the sad mermaid on her rock, then she shook her head.

"But ... but I *can't* help you. I have to save my brother William, and I don't even know where my other brother is, or my ship, *Peregrine*."

"If you help us end the Mermaid Queen's curse, we can help you find your brothers and your ship," he said. Emma hesitated. The figureheads all looked at her with such hopeful expressions. She shifted and frowned.

"Well, why me?"

Finn dropped his voice. "We can only reveal ourselves to someone who has received a gift from the sea."

"Gift? I haven't received any gift from the sea," Emma said, doubtful.

Finn nodded. "Yes, you have. You carry it on your back."

Emma stared at him.

"Your conch shell."

She slowly understood. "You? *You* gave back my shell?"

Finn nodded. "When I took your ensign, in the fog. Who gave it to you anyway? Think back to the day you first found your shell, so long ago, Emma. Did a dolphin leap in the moonlight? Let me see it." Emma reached into her backpack and handed the conch shell to Finn. He raised it to his lips and gently blew. A thin, fine note came out, high and true. It sent shivers down Emma's back. He handed it back to her.

"You can call me with it now, anytime, and I will appear," he smiled.

Emma shook her head. There were too many questions. Finn put seaweed in their mouths to save her and her brothers from *drowning*? He stole their ensign? Now her shell was his doing, too?

It was too much all at once. She still wasn't entirely convinced any of this was real. And how could she possibly help, anyway?

Emma looked at the figureheads. Big mistake. The schoolteacher, the sea captain, the knight and the gladiator, were trying their best to put on a brave face, but Mary-Celeste, being very young, had flopped down in the grass. She handed Emma a daisy-chain.

Her small face was so hopeful. "For you," the little girl said sadly.

Emma uncrossed her arms. She sighed. "Well, what do I have to do?" She wasn't there to break an ancient mermaid curse. She was there because of the phantom ship, the storm, the fog, and running aground. She had to find William and Jonah and get home.

"You have to challenge the Mermaid Queen to break the curse," Finn said quickly.

The figureheads all looked at her. And

for ancient wooden ship statues come to life, Emma thought, they all looked *very* afraid. She was about to say something more, probably something along the lines of *how exactly does one CHALLENGE a mermaid queen* when …

BOOM BOOM da-dum!

BOOM BOOM da-dum!

Everybody jumped. The knight's helmet visor slammed shut. The gladiator drew his short sword. Mary-Celeste whispered, "*Pirates!*"

Emma gulped. "Pirates? There are *pirates* here, too?"

"Oh yes, lassie," the sea captain answered. "And you dinna want to cross them."

"They're not the brightest of pirates, either," the schoolteacher added, as though this explained everything.

BOOM BOOM da-dum!

BOOM BOOM da-dum!

"*Hostibus*," the gladiator breathed, glancing at the treetops.

"That means 'enemy,'" the schoolteacher translated.

"So why are the pirates drumming?" Emma asked, nervously eyeing the treetops with the gladiator.

BOOM BOOM da-dum!

BOOM BOOM da-dum!

"It could be warfare, milady," said the knight helpfully.

"Or perhaps a wee prisoner," the sea captain added.

BOOM BOOM da-dum!
BOOM BOOM da-dum!

"Will you help break the curse, Emma, and set the figureheads free to return to the sea? We've been waiting for someone like you," Finn said. Everybody looked at her, even the sad mermaid.

If it's the only way I can find William and Jonah and our ship, what choice do I have? And none of this is probably real, anyway.

Emma slowly nodded.

"Come on, then," said Finn, handing her the foghorn. "To the Mermaid Queen. Oh, and keep an eye out for the giant snake. He's always hungry."

CHAPTER FOURTEEN

PIRATE JONAH
AT YOUR SERVICE

Jonah held the wheel with his foot. Then he stretched as far as he could and banged the drums.

BOOM BOOM da-dum!
BOOM BOOM da-dum!

He stopped, pulled out a long telescope, and scanned the beach. Emma and William might hear the drums and come to the shore. It was his only plan.

But the beaches stayed empty.

Jonah sailed on, searching the shoreline. He tied a piece of black sailcloth to his head for shade. He shared a banana with the parrot, then it settled on his shoulder with sharp claws and screeched in his ear.

"Pieces of eight! Pieces of eight!"

That'll teach me to be kind, Jonah thought. *And what are pieces of eight, exactly?*

Slowly, Jonah sailed the huge pirate ship to the end of the island. It was hot and tiring work. It was a big ship, a heavy wheel, and the drums were loud. His arms were tired and his head ached. But he couldn't stop until he found his brother and sister.

After a while, the ship reached the end of the island and rounded a point. Jonah saw a lagoon, but he couldn't get too close, since he didn't want to run aground.

He banged the drums.

He looked through the telescope.

Jonah stared hard at the lagoon.

And this time ... *something rose from the water*!

"What *is* that thing? It looks like a disgusting dead fish!" A weird, watery monster-thing loomed above the waves.

AND A BOY was tied to a rock before it! Jonah stared harder. The sun glinted off something in the monster's hand.

Is that ... a boat hook?

"That's not a boy! That's *William*!" Jonah yelled. *But where's Emma?*

"Boil his bones! Shiver me timbers!"

"QUIET, BIRD!" Jonah licked his lips and peered through the telescope. The monster loomed above William, wet and writhing, with a wide-open mouth and a fin down its back. It shook a whalebone sword in one spiny hand and *Peregrine*'s boat hook with the other!

Then the fish-monster pushed William beneath the waves! Jonah raced along the deck. He had to do something!

He ran blindly and then banged into the big black cannon.

Cannonballs sat beside it. And what looked like firecrackers. And a box marked *flints* with long thin matches inside.

How hard could it be?

Jonah hoisted one of the heavy cannonballs into the cannon. He aimed the cannon at the trees — at least he *hoped* he aimed it at the trees. It was hard to tell. He used a flint to light the long wick at the back of the cannon.

The wick sparked and jumped to life. He covered his ears and ducked....

KA-BOOM!

Jonah fell to the deck. For a moment, everything was still. The parrot was still, the ship was still, the trees on the shore were still.

The cannonball sailed across the lagoon.

Jonah *meant* to hit the trees.

He didn't MEAN to wing the fish-monster drowning his brother. He really just meant to scare it off. But he'd never fired a cannon before....

A horrible shriek filled the air. The water rose and boiled where the monster had been, and tentacles and sea-creatures flailed from a wave that rose and rose. The water churned and boiled, higher and higher.

The monster had vanished, but where was William?

And now there was another noise. A weird, watery, burbly screaming. Jonah scanned the water and froze. An army of horrible fish creatures gnashed shark teeth, shook seaweed hair, opened fish lips, and shrieked at him.

"What are *those* things?" he cried. The watery horrors swam toward him. Suddenly, something *thumped* against the boat. He ran to look over the side.

And almost fainted!

The angry fish monsters clung to the pirate ship. Their hands were spiny, and they shook fishbone spears at him. Two of them shook paddles.

Those are Peregrine*'s paddles!*

The creatures clung to every inch of his ship, their slippery green hands clutched every port hole, every knot in the wood. But they couldn't climb out of the water …

… because Jonah saw *fins* where *feet* should be.

Can these things be mermaids? Correction, screaming mermaids!

The sound made Jonah's hair stand up. It made him want to jump overboard and drown himself. Which was perhaps the point.

But, he told himself, *it's just a noise. It can't hurt you if it's just a noise. Try not to listen.*

"Boil his bones! Shiver me timbers! Pieces of eight!" the parrot said over and over. Which was a sudden improvement on the screaming mermaids.

What should I do?

For a moment, pirate Jonah was filled with panic. What if? What if this was all real? What if he wasn't dreaming, but he really lost his brother and sister? What if he *was* all alone, destined to sail a pirate ship around a weird desert island for the rest of his life, with screaming mermaids attached to it?

But then the worst thought of all bubbled to the surface....

What if William drowned?

BUUUUUU! BUUUUUU! BUUUUUU!

Jonah gasped! *That's a foghorn!*

He ran to the side of the ship, swept the telescope along the beach ...

... *Emma and a tall boy ran out of the trees!*

"EMMA!" Jonah shouted. He waved his arms, but he was too far away for his sister to see him. All she'd see was a pirate ship far out at sea.

BUUUUUU! BUUUUUU! BUUUUUU!

Jonah watched through the telescope. Emma blew the foghorn while the tall boy dove into the water. The water writhed and boiled ... then the boy clambered back onto the beach.

He had a boat hook in one hand and *William* in the other! Jonah whooped with joy. William was alive!

Emma and the tall boy ran back into the forest with William between them. Angry mermaids crawled onto the beach, shrieking. Spears fell around Emma, William, and the boy.

BUUUUUU! BUUUUUU! BUUUUUU!

Keep blowing that foghorn, Emma! I'll find you!

Jonah ran to the wheel and turned the pirate ship toward the distant shore. His brother and sister were alive, and he was going to find them, no matter what.

And the army of screaming mermaids was going with him.

CHAPTER FIFTEEN

PLEASE, WILLIAM

Emma and Finn ran across the sand, carrying William between them.

"Lie him down!" Finn said when they were safely under the trees. Angry mermaids shrieked and slapped their tails on the beach behind them, but they couldn't follow.

"Is he okay?" Emma panted and dropped to her knees. Poor William! He looked terrible, pale, and his eyes were closed. Finn kneeled over the boy on the ground.

"He's not ... is he still alive?" Emma whispered. William wasn't breathing. There was no pulse at his neck. Emma felt her heart squeeze.

She *couldn't* lose her big brother! Not here, not now, not yet. *Oh please, not yet!*

She felt a rising panic.

Finn put his hand on the boy's throat. Then he pulled something green from his pocket and placed it on William's tongue. Seaweed.

"It may be too late," Finn said quietly. "Call him, Emma."

"William! Please, William," Emma whispered. She took her brother's hand. It was ice-cold. Finn ran his hand over William's face. He breathed onto the boy's lips. He breathed into his ears and nose. He pressed his hands upon the boy's chest, once, twice, three times. And again and again. Emma stared into William's face.

I will never argue with Jonah again, I promise! Just please wake up!

"Please, William," she whispered again. Her throat was tight, her eyes full of tears. "Wake up! Please!"

"Come, Captain, your sister calls," Finn said softly.

At that moment, William groaned and rolled over. He sat up and rubbed his head. With disgust, he spat seaweed onto his hand.

Emma hugged him.

"What happened? All I remember is the Mermaid Queen," William said, dazed.

Finn helped him up.

"You saved me, Emma. You and your friend here." William looked at Finn carefully. There was something oddly fish-like about the other boy. If he *was* a boy.

"This is Finn." Emma realized she wasn't sure she could explain Finn.

"Pleased to meet you, Captain William Blackwell," Finn answered with a slight bow.

Emma held her brother by the arm. "He's an ancient, wandering sea spirit. He saved you."

"I thought I saw a dolphin save me...." William started, but Finn interrupted him.

"We must go. The pirates wounded the Mermaid Queen, William escaped, and now the mermaids will hunt you all down. You must get to your ship." As though on cue, the distant pirate drums sounded.

BOOM BOOM da-dum!

BOOM BOOM da-dum!

"Come, Blackwells!" Finn trotted away down the path. He clutched *Peregrine*'s boat hook, which looked like a noble weapon in his hands.

"I'll tell you about the dolphin part later," Emma whispered, helping her brother down the pathway.

"Do you know where our brother is? I'm missing a crew member, not to mention my ship," William panted.

"There's no sign of your missing crew. I've found your ship, though...." Finn answered.

They rounded the last turn to the figure-head graveyard. Finn stopped dead, and Emma and William crashed into him.

William's mouth fell open.

There, standing in the middle of the pathway, was the strangest collection of people — if they *were* people — he'd ever seen. Or imagined. The knight, the gladiator, the sad mermaid (who was riding on the horse, with her tail tucked to one side), the sea captain, the schoolteacher and Mary-Celeste all stood under the trees. The monkey chattered above. Emma took a quick look at the bushes along the path — still no sign of the giant snake.

The sea captain stepped forward. "You've done it, lassie! You've broken the curse! We're free!" he said.

Finn shook his head. "No, it wasn't Emma. It was a pirate's cannonball. And the Mermaid

Queen isn't dead, so the curse may not be broken for good." The figureheads exchanged serious glances.

"When did the pirates grow so bold?" the schoolteacher said.

"It *is* strange — usually they are terrified of her," Finn mused. "But now is your chance to be free of the curse forever. We have to battle the Mermaid Queen." Each figurehead nodded solemnly, even little Mary-Celeste.

BOOM BOOM da-dum!
BOOM BOOM da-dum!

"Come on," Finn said. "To *Peregrine* before the pirates find her. Wherever the pirates are, the mermaids will be close behind! And Blackwells, perhaps your missing crew is there, too."

"Emma," William whispered. "What are these … people?"

"They're ancient sea spirits like Finn, except they're cursed and he's not," Emma whispered back.

Of course there would be cursed sea spirits. And pirates, William thought. *If there are monster mermaids, why not pirates, too?*

William tried not to look too closely at the knight and the gladiator as they trotted along the pathway beside them, clanking in their armour. The knight looked at William and bowed slightly.

"Your servant, sir," the knight said. William quickly looked away.

This really couldn't get much weirder!

Emma helped William limp along the pathway, behind the others. She blasted on the foghorn. If Jonah were anywhere near, he'd hear it.

BUUUUUU! BUUUUUU! BUUUUUU!

Ancient figureheads ran and clanked down the path ahead of them. A sad mermaid rode a horse. A monkey chattered in the trees. A strange dolphin-boy brandished a boat hook.

And somewhere nearby, a giant snake slithered quietly along....

CHAPTER SIXTEEN

PEREGRINE, HO!

BOOM BOOM *da-dum!*
    BOOM BOOM da-dum!

Jonah beat the drums. He stuck the pirates' swords in his belt. He stood at the wheel with the parrot on his shoulder and the telescope in his hand as he searched the island.

BUUUUUU! BUUUUUU! BUUUUUU!

Jonah steered toward the sound of Emma's foghorn whenever it came.

There were more and more mermaids around the ship. They bumped along the side; the water was thick with them. An army of angry, shrieking mermaids surrounded him....

BUUUUUU! BUUUUUU! BUUUUUU!

Suddenly, people ran out of the trees and onto the beach!

Jonah peered through the telescope. One of them had a backpack and a foghorn! Another held a boat hook!

"It's them!" he said to the parrot, which was quiet for once. But there was something a little off about the people with Emma and William.

Is that ... a gladiator?

Jonah shook his head.

I must be seeing things! But wait, is that ... a knight?

It was Emma and William all right, but the rest of the people were very odd. If they WERE people. Jonah skimmed the telescope over what looked like a knight, a gladiator, a sea captain with a pipe, and someone — correction, *something* — on a horse. A monkey swung from tree to tree. There was the tall boy in ragged clothes who saved William, clutching the boat hook. A woman in a long black skirt held a little girl's hand. The group ran along the beach just as two dark figures ran out of the trees.

THE PIRATES!

Jonah held the telescope as steady as he could. They were still scary and huge, but the pirates didn't look like zombies anymore. They were Eye-Patch and Gold-Tooth all right, but *real*. The curse must have been broken! They clutched swords from a secret cache buried in the sand and ran toward a *sailboat stuck on the beach.*

It was *Peregrine*!

Emma and her group ran toward the sailboat from one side. And the pirates ran toward the ship from the other. And every second more and more mermaids filled the water between the pirate ship and *Peregrine.*

Who would get to *Peregrine* first?

Jonah jumped back to the wheel. He looked up at the sail. "Come on! Come on!" he yelled at his ship, urging it on.

"Boil his bones!" screeched the parrot on his shoulder.

"I'm going to boil *you* if we don't get to *Peregrine* before those pirates do!"

Jonah sailed on, as fast as he could.

CHAPTER SEVENTEEN

RESCUE AT SEA

William and Emma ran along the beach.

"I can't run much more, Emma," William gasped. The strange day had taken its toll on poor William. Being drowned for part of it didn't help much, either.

"We can't stop now, William! Look!" Emma pointed. "We're almost back at *Peregrine*, and there's a breeze! We can get aboard, then look for Jonah." William rallied, put on a burst of speed and limped as fast as he could, leaning on his little sister.

Finn and the others were far ahead.

Clang! Clang!

Swords clashed down the beach. Finn, the knight, and the gladiator had reached the pirates!

The sea captain stopped for Emma and William. "You must board your ship before the pirates do, bairns. We'll hold them off!" Emma untied *Peregrine*'s red ensign from her backpack and handed it to him.

"Please give this to Finn! A gift from me."

The captain looked surprised, but he nodded.

"Aye, lassie. Hae a guid journey!" Then the good sea captain ran to help the others.

The pirates stabbed and swung their weapons. The gladiator and the knight circled them with their swords. Finn brandished the boat hook. The sea captain, the schoolteacher, and Mary-Celeste shouted encouragement. The monkey chattered in the trees. Coconuts rained down on the pirates' heads.

Then ... a gigantic snake slithered out of the forest. It curled slowly around Gold-Tooth's foot. "YARGH! Sister, the Kraken's got me!" the pirate yelled. The enormous snake tugged the struggling pirate across the sand and into the bushes. Eye-Patch shrieked and ran away along the beach, the pirate and the knight close behind her.

A knight and a gladiator chasing a pirate on a beach. Now there's something you don't see every day, William thought.

Emma dragged William toward *Peregrine*. She'd never been so happy to see their sailboat! Brother and sister slowly pushed the boat out of the soft sand, then they jumped aboard.

BOOM BOOM da-dum!

BOOM BOOM da-dum!

More pirates?

As Emma readied the boat to sail, William grabbed the binoculars. There was a pirate ship all right, and it was heading their way. Between them and the pirate ship, the water frothed and boiled with *mermaids*. William looked closely at the pirate ship. He swept the binoculars across the deck....

JONAH?

William stared. There was no doubt about it. His little brother was at the wheel of the huge black ship, steering right toward them. Jonah even looked like a pirate! He wore a black hat and had swords in his belt. He peered through a telescope, and a green parrot perched on his shoulder.

"Emma! It's Jonah!" William yelled.

Emma grabbed the binoculars. "He's a *pirate!*" she whispered, astonished.

Brother and sister looked at each other. William shrugged.

"We both knew he was always a pirate, deep down. Come on, we'll rescue him at sea!"

Their sails caught the fresh wind. William took the wheel, and the good ship *Peregrine* sailed away from the beach.

This is probably the first time in history that any captain has sailed as fast as they could TOWARD a pirate ship, William thought.

There was a shout in the water behind them.

Finn leapt into the foamy waves. Or was it a dolphin who leapt? Beside him, the horse

shouldered the sea and raced into battle. On his broad back rode the knight and the gladiator. The knight clutched *Peregrine*'s boat hook like a lance.

"Excelsior!" the gladiator cried, brandishing his short sword.

Behind them, the schoolteacher and the sea captain ran across the waves toward the mermaid army. Then came golden-haired Mary-Celeste on the back of the sad mermaid, who was sad no longer. Instead, she looked determined and ferocious. Those other mermaids, the horrible ones, had cursed her and held her captive for a very long time. She, too, was ready for battle.

The figureheads swam and leapt toward the mermaid army.

The war in the waves had begun.

"Sail for your lives, Blackwells!" Finn called. Then he dove, holding the slippery green head of a mermaid. The water was a frothy green sea of slippery heads, tails, and seaweed.

Then ... SHE came! An enormous wave rose in the centre of the battle, filled with sharks, crabs, and fish. The monstrous form of the Mermaid Queen loomed, and with a cry the figureheads fell upon her.

They wanted their freedom.

"We have to help them, William!" Emma cried.

William set his jaw and steadied the wheel. "No, Emma," he said, determined. "Finn told us to *sail for our lives*. We have to save Jonah and get home."

"But they're my friends! I don't want to leave them!"

The water boiled and writhed in the mayhem. Suddenly, Emma saw Finn leap from the waves and raise a conch shell to his lips. The air filled with a long, thin note that made the very waves sing. Again and again, Finn blew into the shell.

"*You* aren't leaving them, Emma," William said, clutching the wheel. "*I* am. Blame *me*. It's my decision. I'm the captain." William had never looked so fierce, or so grown up, as he steered *Peregrine* toward the pirate ship.

Emma watched the war in the waves fall behind them.

Then suddenly, with the leaping forth of a thousand bodies, the dolphins arrived! Finn must have called them with his conch! They looked like Finn — fierce, thin, and tall as they leapt beside him. Now there were almost as many figureheads and wandering sea spirits as there were mermaids, battling in the waves.

The tide had turned! The Mermaid Queen vanished beneath the spray, and her army fled, each mermaid chased by a dolphin — or something that *might* be a dolphin, anyway.

Emma cheered! *Good luck, figureheads*, she thought. *I hope you break the Mermaid Queen's curse and return to the sea forever!*

"Emma, help!" William called, and she turned away from her friends in the sea. She grabbed the life-ring, ready to rescue Jonah....

The pirate ship was close now. Jonah waved frantically from the bow. William steered *Peregrine* as close as he could to the big black ship. Soon the two boats were bow to bow, passing each other quickly. Jonah stood on the railing.

"NOW, JONAH! JUMP!" William shouted. Jonah took off the swords and the hat and then leapt for *Peregrine* with all his might.

He landed on the main sail and rolled into the cockpit. Emma caught him and pulled him to his feet. Jonah looked at his sister and brother, then he looked at his feet.

"Next time, Emma ... I promise I'll catch your shell," Jonah said quietly, looking up.

Emma and William exchanged astonished glances. Then, for the first time in ages, Emma gave her twin a quick hug.

"Welcome aboard, Jonah," William said. That's when Captain William Blackwell of the good ship *Peregrine* actually smiled, his first smile since the whole adventure began.

The drifting pirate ship sailed past. It sailed through the battling mermaids and sea spirits, toward the beach, faster and faster. With a distant crunch and splintering of wood, the pirate ship crash-landed on the beach.

"There goes your ship, Pirate Jonah," Emma said. "And your pirates," she added, as Eye-Patch and Gold-Tooth ran down the beach, chased by the giant snake.

They watched as the green parrot flew into the tall trees. "Boil his bones! Shiver me timbers!"

"Farewell, bird!" Jonah called. He suddenly felt a little sad to see it go. But at least it was free of the zombie pirates.

The war in the waves raged on behind them. Figureheads battled, dolphins leapt, mermaids swam for their lives without their queen, and the good ship *Peregrine* and her crew, together at last, headed out to sea.

CHAPTER EIGHTEEN

THE SEA SPIRIT

Emma woke first.

A heavy fog surrounded the ship.

CLANG. CLANG.

Somewhere in the fog, a harbour buoy rang out. She sat up.

And spat seaweed out of her mouth.

Her brothers slept nearby. Jonah lay on a cockpit bench, and William was slumped over the wheel. They both stirred, woke, and spat seaweed out of their mouths, too.

"Ew," said Jonah.

"How did I get seaweed in my mouth?" William asked. He stretched and rubbed the back of his neck. The thick white fog surrounded them. There was nothing to see. There was no wind. *Peregrine* was becalmed.

"Where are we?" Emma asked.

Jonah got up to look.

"Stuck in this fog."

Suddenly, the marine radio crackled.

"*Peregrine, Peregrine, Peregrine*, this is DaddyOne, over." Jonah scrambled down into the cabin and grabbed the radio. "DaddyOne, DaddyOne, DaddyOne, this is *Peregrine*, over!"

"*Peregrine, Peregrine, Peregrine*, it's good to hear your voice! Is everyone okay? Over." Emma, William, and Jonah looked at each other. William shrugged then nodded.

"DaddyOne, DaddyOne, DaddyOne. Everyone's okay, over," Jonah said. He raised an eyebrow at his brother and sister.

"*Peregrine, Peregrine, Peregrine*, the storm must have knocked out your radio and cellphone for a while. I'm in a tugboat close by. Blow your foghorn now, over."

The three Blackwells looked at each other. Emma raised the foghorn to her lips.

BUUUUUU! BUUUUUU! BUUUUUU!

Soon they could hear the *chug chug* of the tugboat in the fog. Emma blew the foghorn again and again, and then, like a magical beast, the tugboat appeared out of the fog cloud. Jonah threw a line from *Peregrine*, and soon the Blackwells clambered aboard the tug.

After their father hugged each of them and made sure they really were okay, he seemed a little lost for words.

"How did you and *Peregrine* survive the storm, William?" he finally asked.

William shrugged. "It was pretty bad, but we threw out the sea anchor. It helped. We lost it, though." He showed his father the torn line.

"William fell overboard, and Jonah and I had to steer," Emma said.

"But William was a good captain," Jonah added.

"Emma and Jonah were a brave crew. We managed okay," William said.

The Blackwells looked at each other. They *were* a brave crew. William *was* a good captain. They *did* manage okay. There wasn't anything else they could say.

"The motor handle broke, and the jib ripped," William said, scratching his head.

"We lost a few paddles and the boat hook, too," Jonah added. The losses were mounting.

"You lost your ensign?" their father said, squinting up at the top of the mast.

William eyed Emma, who nodded. "Yes, the wind took it during the storm," she said.

"That's never a good sign," their dad said. His children just looked at him. "Well, you know, according to the old sailors."

"No one believes those stories, Dad," Jonah said firmly.

Their father smiled. "Well, you're all right, that's all that matters. We can replace motor handles and boat hooks and ensigns. I'm proud of you. You must have worked together really well to get through the storm." The Blackwells nodded.

Yes. They did.

The tugboat towed *Peregrine* slowly along. They were heading to harbour. It wasn't far, less than an hour by water.

The three sailors sat in the cockpit while their father and the tugboat driver took them to safety. They sat quietly, gently rocking with the waves, their heads nodding with exhaustion, too tired to do anything but look over the water. Soon the fog cleared and the sun sparkled on the waves.

"You made a great pirate, Jonah," Emma whispered sleepily.

"Thank you for blowing the foghorn," he whispered back.

"I have something better than the foghorn," she said. Emma reached into her backpack and pulled out the conch. She raised it to her lips and blew a thin, fine note, high and true. Her brothers both looked impressed.

"Thanks for saving me from the briny deep, too, both of you," William whispered. "But no more talk of mermaids for a while, okay?"

They sat quietly for a while longer.

"Look." Jonah nodded out to sea.

There on the horizon, a bright red flag fluttered above the waves, held in a seaweed-covered hand. Beside it what could only be a boat hook glinted in the sunlight, held by a figure that looked surprisingly like a gladiator astride a horse. And ... was that a *knight*, too?

The boat hook and the flag sank, and a moment later a pod of dolphins leapt into the air. There must have been ten of them or maybe more.

The Blackwells smiled.

Their boat hook and their ensign weren't lost. They were just their gifts to the sea.

Soon, Emma and Jonah fell asleep, leaning on each other. William yawned.

Their father drove the tugboat with his sleeping children, towing *Peregrine* to shore.

And the tugboat's name?

It was, of course, *The Sea Spirit*.

THIS PART IS (ALSO) MOSTLY TRUE

So you've made it to the end of the story. I told you when we started that it was weird and strange and more than a little frightening. You'll probably never look at conch shells the same way or seaweed or even sailboats for that matter.

In fact, this kind of story (and many other sea stories like it) might just be enough to keep you firmly on land for the rest of your life. But that would be a pity. There's nothing like a calm sea and a gentle breeze to bring the sea adventurer to life in all of us.

Still, strange things do happen at sea. And every sailor will tell you hair-raising stories about storms and fog and running aground and people falling overboard. In fact, I'm one of them.

But I suspect what you'd really like to know is this: was the phantom ship *real*? Did Emma and William and Jonah really see one? And did it set them on their strange voyage that day?

Well, there are countless stories of sailors and even people on land — quite sensible people otherwise not given to seeing things — who have seen ghostly ships. The story of a ghost ship is one of the oldest kinds of sea stories and there are stories like it from all over the world.

If you look up *The Flying Dutchman*, for instance, you'll read one of the best-known ghost ship stories of all. The story of the *Mary-Celeste* is a pretty scary tale, too.

So it's entirely possible that the Blackwells saw a phantom ship that day. Plenty of sailors claim they have, more experienced and much older sailors than them.

But you're probably also wondering about Finn. Well, again, all I can tell you is that there are plenty of stories about dolphins saving drowning sailors. Plus, there are sailors who believe that ship figureheads hold sea spirits (also known as *kaboutermannekes* in Dutch sailing lore) who lead lost sailors to safety.

As for the seaweed in the mouth, well, why not?

And the strange, enchanted island? All I can say on that score is that *all* sea stories lead somewhere, some to white whales, some to buried pirate's treasure, some to lonely castaways, and some even lead to enchanted islands. (Mr. Shakespeare has a wonderful shipwrecked-sailors-on-an-enchanted-island story, for instance.)

Finally, what about the pirates and mermaids? Well, almost any sea story worth its salt has a pirate in it. And many of them have mermaids, too. (A famous sailor named Odysseus met some interesting mermaids.)

But more than all of that, I suspect you're wondering about the Blackwells. Did they really have all those adventures that day? Well, true or not, they had a gripping sea story to share together for the rest of their lives. A good story is a good story, after all, and a good *sea story* is one of the best stories of all, in my opinion.

And I can tell you this, too: after their adventure at sea, the Blackwells rarely quarrelled again. Together they survived a phantom ship, a terrible storm, a fog bank, possible drowning, zombie pirates, and monster mermaids. They befriended cursed figureheads and a wandering sea spirit on a shipwreck island, too. All that does something to a family.

In fact, the Blackwells grew closer and closer with age.

There were only two things that were a little strange about them.

One: at family gatherings, the three of them would always retire to a corner after dinner with a conch, a foghorn, and a boat hook. They talked quietly among themselves, late into the night, shooing everyone else away. Their children, and then many years later, their grandchildren, would sneak close and catch the words "Finn" and "Mermaid Queen" and something that sounded like crab-outer-manatees, but probably wasn't.

Two: if you ever asked one of them to go for a sail, they'd get deadly serious, pull you close, and whisper, "But does your boat have a *figurehead*?"

SAILING GLOSSARY

Aground: any boat stuck on land is "aground"

Becalmed: a sailboat without wind

Boat hook: a long pole with a hook

Boom: attached to the mast at right angles, the boom holds the bottom of the main sail

Bow: the front of a boat

Brigantine: an old-fashioned, two-masted sailing vessel

Bunk: bed, in the cabin

Buoy: a marker for safe passage into a harbour, sometimes with a bell or light

Cabin: the covered portion of a sailboat, for sleeping, cooking, and shelter

Cockpit: the outside area of a sailboat, used for steering and navigation

Dock: a bridge from land to boat

Ensign: the ship's flag

Figurehead: a carved wooden statue on the bow of old sailboats, to bring luck or to strike fear, sometimes believed to harbour sea spirits (see *Kaboutermanneke*)

First mate: second in command, below the captain

Flotsam: wreckage floating from a sunken vessel

Foresail: sail at the front of the boat (not the main sail)

Galley: kitchen, in the cabin

Gang-plank: a board placed over the side of the sailboat, usually over the water

Halyard: any rope or wire used to pull the sails up or down

Handrail: a sturdy rail on top of the cabin, for crew safety

Hanging locker: a closet in the cabin

Head: bathroom, in the cabin

Jib: small foresail

Jolly Roger: the pirate's flag, sometimes with a skull, crossed bones, or swords

Kaboutermanneke: a helpful, wandering sea spirit, sometimes believed to be found in wooden figureheads in Dutch sailing lore (see *Figurehead*)

Lifeline: fixed ropes or wires for safety aboard a boat

Life-ring: a life-saving flotation device kept at hand to toss to sailors in the water

Line: any rope used to tie the boat to shore or another boat

Main sail: the biggest sail on the sailboat, attached to the main mast

Mast: a tall vertical post (wooden or metal), which holds the main sail, boom, and halyards

Overboard: swept off the ship into the water

Phantom ship: a ghostly ship at sea, which appears and vanishes in moments

Ready-about: the captain's orders to prepare the sailboat to turn across the wind and change direction

Scuppers: pipes or gutters to drain water

Sea anchor: a large net-like bag attached to the boat, dragged in the water for stability in a storm

Sheet: any rope used to control the sails

Ship log: a journal kept by the captain or crew, telling the ship's position and events

Stern: the back of a boat

Wheel: sailboat steering system aboard the *Peregrine*

They're troubling. They're bizarre.
And they JUST might be true …

Weird Stories Gone Wrong

BY PHILIPPA DOWDING
ILLUSTRATED BY SHAWNA DAIGLE

JAKE AND THE
GIANT HAND (2014)
The ghastly truth about
a giant hand …

MYLES AND THE
MONSTER OUTSIDE (2015)
A rainy night, a haunted highway,
a mysterious monster …

CARTER AND THE
CURIOUS MAZE (2016)
Are you brave enough to
enter the curious maze?
Not everyone comes out …

ALEX AND THE OTHER (2018)
An evil twin, a haunted mirror, and strangers who whisper … *BEWARE THE OTHER!*

BLACKWELLS AND THE BRINY DEEP (2018)
Shrieking mermaids, zombie pirates, an enchanted island, and *do you hear the distant drums?*

Weird Stories Gone Wrong

FIVE TREMENDOUSLY TERRIFYING TALES YOU'LL WANT TO SHARE WITH YOUR FRIENDS (SHOULD YOU WANT TO SCARE THEM SILLY).

#WeirdStoriesGoneWrong

More Books by Philippa Dowding

The Strange Gift of Gwendolyn Golden

Book 1 in the Night Flyer's Handbook series

This morning, I woke up on the ceiling ...

So begins the strange story of Gwendolyn Golden. One perfectly ordinary day for no apparent reason, she wakes up floating around her room like one of her little brother's Batman balloons.

Puberty is weird enough. Everyone already thinks she's an oddball with anger issues because her father vanished in a mysterious storm one night when she was six. Then there are the mean, false rumours people are spreading about her at school. On top of all that, now she's a flying freak.

How can she tell her best friend or her mother? How can she live her life? After Gwendolyn almost meets disaster flying too high and too fast one night, help arrives from the most unexpected place. And stranger still? She's not alone.

**Everton Miles Is
Stranger Than Me**

Book 2 in the Night Flyer's
Handbook series

*I wander around like any normal
self-absorbed teenager. Do we all think we're being
chased by deadly entities? Probably, but how many
of us actually are?*

Gwendolyn Golden, Night Flyer, floats over the cornfields all summer. What draws her to the same spot, night after night? All she knows is that change is coming: she's starting high school *plus* there's a strange new boy in town.

He's Everton Miles and he's a Night Flyer, too.

Soon the mismatched teenagers face dangers they never imagined, including a fallen Spirit Flyer, a kidnapping, and the eternal darkness of The Shade. How will Gwendolyn handle her new life *and* grade nine? With help from *The Night Flyer's Handbook* and her strange new friend, it might not be that hard.

*CCBC's Best Books for Kids & Teens
(Spring 2017) Selection*